D1436034

THE SPEAK OF THE MEARNS

THE SPEAK OF THE MEARNS

Lewis Grassic Gibbon

THE RAMSAY HEAD PRESS · EDINBURGH

First published in 1982 by
The Ramsay Head Press
36 North Castle Street
Edinburgh EH2 3BW

Printed in Great Britain by
John G Eccles Printers Ltd

The publisher acknowledges the
financial assistance of the
Scottish Arts Council in the
publication of this volume.

CONTENTS

INTRODUCTION

When he died suddenly in February 1935, James Leslie Mitchell, better known by his pseudonym Lewis Grassic Gibbon, was hard at work at a rate which would have left most authors gasping — but which enabled him to achieve what he did in the hectically brief writing period he lived to enjoy. Novels, essays, science fiction, journalism, published papers on archaeology, cultural history, popular science — everything was grist to Gibbon's mill, and his working papers are full of plans and unfinished schemes. He was a man at the peak of his powers, long denied the chance to write through poverty and the force of circumstances. Once the dam broke, it seemed nothing could stop him. *Sunset Song* established his reputation in 1932. On both sides of the Atlantic, he was a man who busied himself to become published, to become known. Infectiously friendly, yet shrewdly able to capitalise on friendships, he seemed set for success. His sudden death from peritonitis cut short a flood of projects. The novella which follows was one of these.

II

James Leslie Mitchell was born in Aberdeenshire, in Auchterless in 1901. His family moved, in much the same way as Chris Guthrie's in *Sunset Song*, South by stages to Bloomfield in Arbuthnott parish. There, in the Howe of the Mearns, his father crofted and brought up his family in fairly straitened circumstances. Leslie was an outwardly undistinguished crofter's son, short, dark, very self-possessed. He worked on the farm as little as he could, day-dreamed constantly, sneaked off from farming duties as soon as possible. He cycled endlessly round the country-side as he grew older, and buried himself in books. He began to be distinguishable from his contemporaries when the books, and the friends he made, led him to emulate a lifestyle he did not yet know at first hand. He improved his speech and his manners; he adopted city ways and mixed less and less with his Arbuthnott contemporaries. At school he read, alone, during breaks and ceased to join in the sports. His passionate interest in archaeology took him to the Manse where he found a fellow-enthusiast in the Minister; his passionate interest in books was fostered and developed by Alexander Gray, the sensitive schoolmaster who encouraged him. As the adventures of the semi-autobiographical Malcom Maudslay in *The Thirteenth Disciple* make clear, Arbuthnott could not contain the explod-ing interests of a Leslie Mitchell who saw in it a foreground of often hated trivial domestic duties, but a background of historical association, archaeological remains, dim sugges-tions of a Scotland which existed in books and historical legend, not in the prosaic reality of Arbuthnott.

A fortunate bursary to Mackie Academy, Stonehaven, gave Leslie his one year of secondary schooling. Expelling himself through disgust with the conformist and old-fashioned educational methods he found there (he was never one to suffer the shortcomings of others gladly), the author moved first to Aberdeen as a trainee reporter, then to Glasgow as a travelling journalist. An eager Marxist, a rebel against many of his family's values of Christian conformity, he made himself unpopular by repeated refus-al to "come home" and settle to a country existence. The failure of journalism, a clumsy attempt at suicide, the derision of his family and friends drove him to a move so desperate as to indicate his poverty and depression. Enlist-ing in the forces, at different times in the Army and Air Force, he spent years as a clerk loathing the proximity of his fellow-soldiers, but enjoying travel which took him to the Middle East, and enjoying the time to write his first short stories.

Marriage to the girl he had known from the farm next door in Arbuthnott, and years of poverty-stricken struggling in London and Welwyn Garden City, led him slowly but successfully to establishing a literary career. From short stories he moved to a number of semi-autobiographical novels (*The Thirteenth Disciple* was republished in 1981) and some intriguing fiction based on his historical and scientific interests — particularly *Spartacus* (1933), a superior and well-informed study of an unpleasant period of history. Slowly, commercial success brought security, travel, time to study in the British Museum, the relaxation of friends and the respect of contemporaries of the stature of Wells. What this success did not bring was reconciliation with Arbuthnott. His family could not or would not understand the wellsprings of his inspiration, the love-hate relation in his memory to the land of his earliest recollection. To them the acerbic views of *Sunset Song* were not at all a laughing matter, but the sharp cause of offence in the community they still inhabited. They had become, they complained, "the speak of the Mearns". It has taken decades for *A Scots Quair* to reach popularity in the Mearns which inspired it, and whose memory haunts the autobiographical essays in *Scottish Scene* (1934). Leslie Mitchell could not return in triumph to Kinraddie to claim his reward of popularity. He returned in semi-disgrace to an unhappy and hostile family, and he was glad to return to a Welwyn Garden City which, increasingly, was becoming home. Like Stevenson in Samoa, he was writing of a country from which he was in exile, even though it occupied the forefront of his imagination insistently.

With his death, his literary career seemed blighted. Only the loyal advocacy of a few friends, and the persistence of his widow, kept his name in the public eye, and publication and republication of his work has been slow. Recently, with television adaptations, mass popularity has come, in North America and in Europe. Ironically, Ray Mitchell is not longer alive to see the success she fought for. Yet the papers she methodically preserved are now available for study in the National Library of Scotland, and in that way this novella has come to light, and to first full publication.

III

The Mearns today is decisively different from the sheltered byeways of Lewis Grassic Gibbon's boyhood. That is a primary theme of the sunset image in *Sunset Song*. With the cutting of the trees on his farm, Chae Strachan sees finally that the old pattern of agriculture will never be re-established. Short-term war needs may claim his trees, but their shelter will take generations to replace. Similarly, Chris's brother Will scoffs at the idea of coming back after the War to a community "dead or dying" like Kinraddie, and by implication his view is shared by the other men who find the enlargement of experience offered even by wartime service in Europe an escape from the stifling narrowness of life on the crofts, living in bothies a communal existence which denied them width of vision or fullness of life. Chris sees Chae and Rob and Ewan killed, but she sees also the death of their community. The war memorial is unveiled to a threnody which is less about the men who died, than about the future which the peace of 1918 ushered in. In *Cloud Howe*, revisiting her earlier years in Kinraddie, Chris finds it all but unrecognisable. Mechanisation and enclosure have made the once-tight community of small farms part of a large and relatively shapeless agricultural district. *Sunset Song* is indeed, as its last paragraphs indicate, about "the last of the peasants".

The process is much advanced in the 1980s. If small farms were threatened by the financial pressures of 1918, they are all but extinct now, Lewis Grassic Gibbon's childhood home is a private house, its land swallowed up by larger neighbours. The tight community of shops and houses, school and Church is much diminished, the school closed, the local services revolutionised by the private car. The quality of life is less distinctively that of Kinraddie, the land part of a larger local unit.

Yet it remains tantalisingly, visibly, the land of *A Scots Quair*. To drive from Montrose towards Stonehaven is to pass evocative signs, pointing to the names Chris knew in her youth in *Sunset Song*; first Johnshaven, then Gourdon, then Bervie which was the market town for Blawearie, the town where the doctor lived, where the spinning-mills worked. Northwards still is Kinneff where the foghorn Chris could hear from her farm still blows, then comes Catterline with its artists' colony, before the road descends to Stonehaven, passing the ruins of Dunnottar Castle unchanged since the time when Chris in the novel was courted by her husband at the foot of the cliffs there.

To turn inland at Bervie, to drive up the river, is to drive back in time to the countryside of *Sunset Song*. At first impression, little has changed. The ancient thirteenth-century Church stills stands by the river, the Manse behind it (partly inspiring the setting of *Cloud Howe*) still surrounded by its trees. Inside the Church the stained glass windows still exactly match the description of the novel, and nearby Arbuthnott House still stands, a reminder of the dominant pattern of local landowning. But the school has closed, the shops are fewer, the buses gone. Bloomfield is a private house, and the work of the farms is almost entirely mechanised.

From his geographical and emotional distance, Gibbon could see all this happening in the 1920s and 1930s. Then as now there must have been a short-lived sense, on arrival, that nothing has changed. But homecoming must have been continuously a process of adjustment, different faces, small farms gone, old people dead, new ways of doing things. As such, the tension between Arbuthnott past and Arbuthnott present must have been a continuous challenge

11

to his creative talent.

Two paths, certainly, lay open to him. One was to write *about change*, and this is what he managed to do in *A Scots Quair*. There is no turning back for Chris, as experience pushes her to womanhood and tragedy, the loss of mother followed by the loss of her father, her husband, the other members of her family, Chae, Rob — she knows she cannot go home again to the security of youth. For this reason, the novel climaxes on the unveiling of the war memorial, the troubling effect of the piper playing his age-old lament which none can understand, yet none can resist. Chris and the bystanders alike are troubled by "The Flowers o the Forest", but the words the minister speaks trouble them too. They are not about the dead, they are about the future — and they echo the author's whole thrust in writing about Scotland in *A Scots Quair*. Chris is propelled by her author from the country to the small town, from the small town to the city. A woman living in un-emancipated times, she is propelled to marriage after marriage to survive, to gain social acceptance. Her only surviving child grows up not to sustain her, but to leave her at the end of *Grey Granite* to pursue his vision as she pursues hers — Ewan to London to a Marxist future, Chris to Benachie and some reunion with her native Scotland.

But if Gibbon destroyed the ground behind him as he followed his characters through the 1920s, he had another artistic resource open to him. This gave the present novella its inspiration; Gibbon could turn from Arbuthnott to the adjacent countryside and parishes to cover fresh territory, moving East to the coast, past Bervie Brow and Craig David, and down to the sea at Kinneff where Little Johnshaven and its cliff stand as a reminder of the old fishing families, where the Old Kirk of Kinneff (recently restored as a historical monument) stands, with its manse, little changed for over a century.

Kinneff seems to give impetus to the imagined territory of this novel, though plainly it is not an exact picture, nor is it bounded by the territory of Kinneff — for instance, the

12

school scenes towards the end of the fragment seem clearly to have come from the author's memory of Arbuthnott School. But the roadside community with its Free Kirk, and the scattered farms towards the sea, surrounding the Old Kirk at the foot of its hill, echo strongly the memory of Kinneff and its surroundings. Typically, Gibbon is mixing memory with fantasy.

In *Sunset Song*, Gibbon made much of the history of Dunnottar Castle and the bravery which saw the smuggling out of the Scottish Regalia from the besieged castle in 1651. The Minister of Kinneff and his wife took the smuggled jewels by night, round by the sea, and they remained safe buried beneath the floor of Kinneff Old Kirk till the siege was lifted, and the invaders had gone. Young James Leslie Mitchell, who cycled the Mearns excitedly in search of history and archaeology, would have rejoiced to have this incident on his doorstep to weave into the fabric of his novel. The area, in truth, is rich in such stimulus to the young mind, standing stones (several sets obviously contributed to the *motif* he chose to highlight in *Sunset Song*), ancient graves, ruined castles. One such castle stood, identifiable at least in the outlines of its walls, near the Old Kirk of Kinneff till quite recent times. But like the personalities which might have fired the author's imagination, that castle has largely disappeared. Time has smoothed out the countryside, and the forces of change have largely eliminated the small farms and the close agricultural fabric of society which was Kinraddie. Today the motor car and the larger mechanised farm have transformed the Mearns, but something of the character Gibbon remembered from London remains. The texture of *The Speak of the Mearns* is typical: affectionate, acerbic, pin-sharp.

There are echoes of work outside Gibbon's own: perhaps the most obvious is to D.H. Lawrence and the world of *Sons and Lovers* (or indeed some of the short stories). There are echoes from his own life, from the details we know in the letters and the proposed "Memoirs of a Materialist" with which he was to approach his own autobiography, and from the early experiments in fiction such as *The Thirteenth Disciple* and *Stained Radiance*, the evocation of the strong family bond, the extraordinary character of the author's mother, the source of his pseudonym and much besides. Lilias Grassic Gibbon in real life was the motive force in Gibbon's family, her strong character and business sense offset by a more silent or reserved husband; if John Guthrie dominates in *Sunset Song*, his character in this sketch is softened and rounded, and the weaker son naturally looks to the mother in whose company he perforce spends so much time.

The son who is of the farm but not part of its workforce, the shy sensitive boy who finds school such an adventure after the experiences of farm life, the young reader on the verge of the world of books, the hypersensitive record of farming life in its incident and linguistic virtuosity — these are the patterns of Gibbon's own youth. Had he lived to continue this story, he would no doubt have carried it into the rector's class at the school, into nearby Duncairn with its academy, and into some variation of the adult experience which is Malcom Maudslay's, or even Chris Guthrie's. This is a variation of the subtitle of *Stained Radiance: A Fictionist's Prelude*. Its value is two-fold. One is the sharpness of its presentation of local life, in a technique now fully developed, a character or incident pinned in a memorable phrase. The other component of its value lies in the more direct autobiographical experience the mature writer can give his own, masculine, persona. Chris Guthrie, memorable as her childhood is in *Sunset Song*, is metamorphosed into a girl. While her author may have chosen not to mix with the other boys in his school environment, he did not much mix with the girls either. Much of Chris's life is imaginary, no matter how exact the setting. With the present pages, we seem to enter the experience of the author himself, compounded from remembered incident, observed from just the distance here imputed to sickness, but in real life arising from shyness and distaste for the farm life.

14

IV

The beginning of the story of Maiden Castle and its inhabitants is defective. The surviving typescript lacks several of the first pages, and is continuously available from page 7 only. On the other hand, it has a number of working notes which are reproduced as an appendix at the end, and it also had the author's first draft of a map which closely confirms much of the guesswork someone familiar with the area could make concerning real-life similarities to the farms depicted. Gibbon was fond of drawing maps, and each of the three books of *A Scots Quair* had a map by himself in the early editions, mostly an accurate and attractive confirmation of local geography, but always containing just enough distortion and invention to throw off the scent any reader seeking to "prove" that the novels were too exactly, or too libellously, based on life. The map confirms the settling of the novel in the area from the roadside of Kinneff to the Old Kirk and the seacoast around; the working papers confirm what might have been Gibbon's intentions in continuing the novel.

It seems quite wrong to do more than present, very lightly edited, what Gibbon wrote. To write an end for this novella, even from the author's skeleton plans, would be to compromise the achievement of this economical first part. To flesh in the early pages is unnecessary to anyone familiar with the brilliant opening pages of *Sunset Song*. The early pages are a confirmation of what we know about the author's developed view of history and society, amply detailed in his sardonic sketches of Scotland in *Scottish Scene* (1934); these pages begin in a Scotland which has inherited the blight of centuries of misrule and exploitation by a "boss" class hated by Gibbon the Marxist and Gibbon the Diffusionist. To him the only true existence is the freedom of human beings who have never known religion, society, law or the other banes of civilisation forced on a free human band by centuries of exploitative history. The world of Chris's Standing Stones in *Sunset Song*, or of pre-civilisation freedom in *Three Go Back* is closer to the ideal, cruel and abrupt as it can be without warning. Gibbon hated the depths to which he thought his country had been plunged by the Great War, by the greedy landlords, by the international Depression which had driven trade and farming to new levels of penny-pinching and discomfort. He had lived close to the poverty line himself in Arbuthnott, and all his later studies led him to attribute that discomfort to historical forces rapidly leading towards the explosion of a Marxist revolution, and the re-establishment of freedom, in some new version, for all the people of Scotland.

This, in outline, is the revolutionary belief behind the shape of *A Scots Quair*, and clearly it is implicit in the incidents planned for this novel, showing as they do the disintegration of society, the institutions and religious observance of a tight community. The Sunset of Chris's life was reflected by the end of an era, and the emotional appeal of this book as a whole would clearly have been different from the *naïveté* of these early years.

V

Gibbon wrote these pages at speed, and his uncertainty is reflected in hasty typing, manuscript changes, changes of mind about names ("The Howe" becomes the slightly less recognisable, more sardonic "The Howl"), signs of work-in-progress. We know from his surviving papers that he had several novels in his mind, some Scottish, some not. There is the start of a Scottish novel quite unconnected with this, and there are clear indications that he intended a novel on the Covenanters (*Men of the Mearns*), a novel on a non-Scottish theme, and a "Scottish" novel which was being actively offered to publishers, though Gibbon pardonably exaggerated the extent to which it was nearing completion when he was engaged on the hectic work-schedule of the last winter of his life.

The New Year of 1935 brought prolonged gastritis, depression, inability to work. He had had a number of advances for work only partly written or not even begun, his schedule of publications was pressing. We know he kept two typewriters in steady use, apart from employing a typing agency to produce fair copy for publishers. This typescript is his own, corrected in his own hand. The sudden break suggests a project so far confined to the privacy of his study, work very much in progress. The style suggests no falling-off from the achievement of *A Scots Quair*, nothing to suggest the work of a sick man.

What we may guess is that in the Winter of 1934/35, Gibbon had a Scottish novel in progress, and that either pressure of an imminent press-date forced him to break off to turn to another project (which he had certainly had to do before), or a sudden attack of illness forced him to lay it aside meantime, without trying to write through an illness which would have diminished the quality of the prose.

Parts of the typescript have been already published, in *A Scots Hairst* ed. I.S. Munro (Hutchinson, 1967), 247-60. That text here is reproduced by permission of the publishers, and the remainder by permission of Mitchell's daughter Mrs Rhea Martin, and with the kind co-operation of the present owners, the National Library of Scotland. Three other debts are due: to the Scottish Arts Council, whose generosity made the publication possible, to Mrs Ray Mitchell who so meticulously preserved her husband's papers till they could be published or re-published, and to Gibbon's contemporary and schoolfriend Gerald Bannerman of Inverbervie, whose help in the editor's study of Lewis Grassic Gibbon has been invaluable.

November, 1982   Ian Campbell

*Sketch map of the area
from Lewis Grassic Gibbon's
notebook*

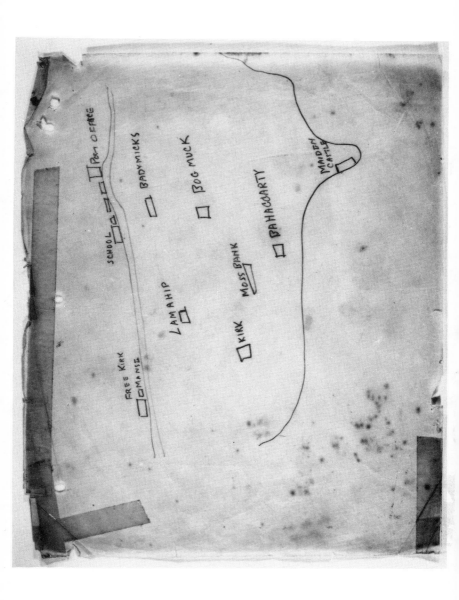

19

BOOK I

When the Romans came marching up into Scotland away far back in the early times they found it full up of red-headed Kerns with long solemn faces and long sharp swords, who rode into battle in little carts, chariots they called them, of wicker and wire, things pulled by small ponies that galloped like polecats and smelt the same, scythes on the hubs; and the deeper they marched up through the coarse land and less they liked it, the Italian men. And by night they'd sit down inside their camps and stare at the moving dark outside, whins and broom, hear the trill of some burn far off going down through Scotch peats to the sea, and wish to their heathen Gods that they'd bidden at home, not wandered up here. And next morning they'd dig some more at the camp and pile up great walls and set up a mound and mislay a handful or so of pennies and a couple of bracelets and a chamber pot to please the learned of later times, and syne scratch their black Italian heads and make up their minds to push further north.

Well, the further they got up beyond the low lands the wilder and coarser the wet lands turned, the Caledonians had wasted the country and burned their crops and hidden their goats far up in the eyries, even sometimes their women, though women weren't nearly so valuable as goats, all that you needed to breed a fresh woman was a bed and a loan of your neighbour's wife, long faced and solemn as yourself. So the Romans jabbered at the women they got, and built more camps and felt home-sick for home, Rome, and its lines of wine shops, till they came in the lour of a wet autumn day up through the Forest of Forfar, dark, pines lining the dripping hills in a sweat, and saw below them the Howe of the Mearns, along dreich marsh that went on and on and was sometimes a loch and sometimes a bog, the mountains towered north, snow on their heights eastwards, beyond the ledge of more hills, came the grumble and southwards girn of the sea . . .

. . . their creash into the red Mearns clay as it well became the lowly-born, pointed by God to serve the gentry.

By then the long Howe was drying up, here and there some little tenant of the lords would push out a finger of corn in the swamps, and dry and drain and sweat through a life-time clearing the whins and the twined bog roots, working his wife and bairns to the bone, they'd not complain, there wasn't time, from morn to night the fight would go one, at the end of a life time or thereabouts another three acres would be hove from the marsh and a man would be easing his galluses, crinkled and bent and half-blind, and just be ready to go a slow stroll and take a look at the work of his life: and the canny Mearns lairds would come riding up "Oh, ay? You've been reclaiming land here?" And the tenant would give them a glower, "Ay." "Then you know that all lands reclaimed in this area belongs to the manor?" And the tenant if he had any wisdom left from the grind and chave of his sweating day would 'gree to that peaceful and pay more rent; if he didn't he was chased from the land he held and hounded south and out of the county, maybe strayed to Fife and was seized on there and held a slave in the Fifshire mines, toiling naked him and his wife and bairns, unpaid, unholidayed in the long half-dark. For that was the Age of God and King when Scotland had still her Nationhood.

And here and there a village rose, with a winding street and a line of huts, each fronted by a bonny midden-pile, along the coast rose St Cyrus, Johnshaven, Bervie, Stonehaven, Stonehaven's middens the highest and feuchest, in the days of the Spanish Armada a lone and battered ship of that fleet crept up the North Coast on a foggy night, the Santa Catarina, battered and torn; and maybe she'd have escaped to her home and her crew got back to their ordinary work of selling onions up and down the streets but that she came within smell of Stonehaven and sank like a stone with all hands complete.

But about the times of the Killing Time the castle of Dunnottar was laid seige by the English, men of that creature Cromwell came up, him that had warts on his nose and his conscience, and planted great bombards against Dunnottar where the crown and the sceptre of Scotland were hidden. And George Ogilvie was the childe in command, he said he wouldn't surrender, not him, though the heavens fell and the seas should yawn, he was ready to sacrifice his men, the castle, the land, Kinneff itself, rather than yield an inch to Cromwell. And the English, aye soft-headed by nature, prigged at him to yield, they didn't want blood, only the crown and the sceptre, that was all. But while they were prigging he'd those fairlies lifted and carted off to another place, the minister's wife, Mrs Grainger hid them, carting them off in the hush of one night to the Headland of the Howe, soft laplap went the sea in the dusk as she rowed the boat in under a crumbling wall and ruined dyke lone and pale in the light of the moon, here Maiden Castle once had arisen. And as she climbed up the eyrie track and over the long deserted walls, something moved queer in her heart at the sight, she turned and looked from the walls to the sea and the moon sinking low and wan; and made up her mind she would mind that place till the time she died.

She did the minding before that came. The English grew tired of besieging Dunnottar and brought up their bombards and trained them and fired them; and George Ogilvie gave a skirl of fear and surrendered at once and the English came in and ransacked Dunnottar from top to bottom, not a trace of the regalia stuff; and not a trace had any for years, till the Restoration came and the King and the Graingers howked the regalia stuff from the place where it had lain under the floor of the kirk; and when they came to ask for reward Mrs Grainger asked that she have the land where Maiden Castle stood by the sea.

Now the Grainger woman had been a Stratoun, she was

23

big and boney with black thick hair, a bit like a horse, only not so bonny, and she planned to settle her goodson Grant in Maiden Castle, could they get it re-built, and plough up the tough land on the landward side and get him to do a bit fishing or smuggling or stealing or a bit of pirating and keep himself in an honest way. So with the little she'd saved in her life, her man the minister a fusionless old gype mooning and dreaming and thinking of God and rubbish like that instead of getting on, she set up Grant in Maiden Castle, they built a fine Scotch farm-house, half that and half a laird's hall it was; and Grant she had alter his name to Stratoun; and there was laid the beginning of folk who sweated a three hundred years in that parish douce and well-spoken, if maybe a bit daft. The littlest of lairds in changing Kinneff, they would lift their heads as the years and the generations went by and see changes in plenty come on the land, it broadened out from the old narrow strips into the long parks for the iron plough, horse-ploughing came and at last a road, driving betwixt Bervie and Stonehaven, filled with the carriages of the gentry folk; and here and there a new farm would rise, to spoil the lands of the little crofters. And by then Kinneff had two kirks of its own, and a schoolhouse and a reputation as a home for liars so black it would have made a white mark on charcoal.

Stonehaven had grown the county town, a long dreich place built up a hill, below the sea in a frothing bay, creaming; and its had a fair birn of folk in it by then, bigger it had grown than any other Mearns place, even Laurence-kirk with its trade and its boasting; and a Stonehaven man would say to a Laurencekirk man: "Have you got a Provost in Laurencekirk man?" and the Laurencekirk childe would say "Aye, that we have; and he's chains." And the Stonehaven gype would give a bit sniff, "Faith, has he so? Ours runs around loose."

Bervie had mills and spinners by then when the eighteen eighties opened up; and it was fell radical and full up of souters ready to brain you with a mallet or devil if you spoke a word against that old tyke Gladstone. It lay back from the sea in a little curve that wasn't a bay and wasn't straight coast and in winter storms the sea would come up, frothing and gurling through a souter's front door and nearly swamp the man setting by his fire, with the speeches of Gladstone grabbed in one hand and Ingersoll under his other oxter.

Now these were nearly the only towns that the folk of the Howe held traffic with, they'd drive to them with the carts for the market, cattle for sale, and bonny fat pigs, grain in the winter, horses ploughing through drifts, and loads of this and that farm produce. And outside it all was an antrin world, full of coarse folk from the north and south.

THE HOWE

I

Now here was the line of the curling coast, a yammer of seagulls night and day, the tide came frothing and swishing green into the caves that curled below; and at night some young-like ploughman childe, out from his bothy for seagull's eggs, swinging and showding from a rope far down would hear the dreich moan of the ingoing waters and cry out to whoever was holding the rope: "Pull me up, Tam. The devil's in there."

But folk said the devil maybe wasn't so daft as crawl about in the caves of The Howe when he could spend a couthy night in the rooms and byres of Maiden Castle, deserted this good ten years or more, green growing on the slates and a scurf from the sea grey on the windows and over the sills. The last Stratoun there had been the laird John who drank like a fish, nothing queer in that, a man with a bit of silver would drink, what else was there for the creature to do if he was a harmless kind of man? But as well as that his downcome had been that he swam like some kind of damned fish as well, he was always in and out of the sea and the combination had been overmuch, one night his son, John was going to bed when he heard far low down under the wall a cry like a lost soul smored in hell. He waited and listened and thought it some bird, and was just about to crawl under the sheets, douce-like, when the cry rose shrill again. It was summer and clear, wan all the forward lift over the sea; and as young John Stratoun ran down the stairs he cried to his mother "There's a queer sound outside. Rouse the old man."

His mother cried back the old devil wasn't in his bed to rouse but out on some ploy, John should leave him a-be, he'd come on all right, never fear the devil aye heeded to his own. And with that the coarse creature, a great fat wretch, she could hardly move for her fat, folk said, a

Murray quean, they aye run to creash, turned over and went off in a canny snooze. The next thing she know was John shaking her awake. "Mother, it's faither and I'm feared he's dead."

So she got from her bed with a bit of a grunt and went down and inspected the corpse of her man, ay, dead enough, blue at the lips, he'd filled himself up with a gill of Glenlivet and gone for a swim, and been taken with cramp. And folk told that the Stratoun woman said "Feuch! You were never much, Sam lad, when you were alive and damn't, you're not even a passable corpse."

But folk in the Howe would tell any lies, they'd a rare time taking the news through hand, Paton at the Mains of Balhaggarty said the thing was a surely a judgement, faith on both the coarse man and his coarse-like wife, the only soul he was sorry for was the boy. And at that the minister to whom he was speaking, nodded his head and said "Ay. You're right. Then no doubt you'll have no objections, Mr Paton, to contributing a wee thing for the creature's support? They've been left near without a penny-piece." So Paton pulled a long sad face and had to dig out, and it served him well.

They didn't bide long in the place after that, the stock and the crops and the gear in the castle were rouped at the end of the Martinmas, the Stratoun woman would have rouped Maiden Castle as well but she couldn't, it descended to John the son. So instead she left the place stand as it was, no tenant would take it, and went off to the south, Montrose, or foreign parts like that, to keep the house for her brother there him that was a well-doing chandler childe. And sleep and rain and the scutter of rats came down on Maiden and there had bidden for a good ten years, till this Spring now came, a racket of silence hardly broken at all but that now and then on a Sunday night when the minister was off to his study for prayer and the elders prowling the other side of the parish and the dogs all locked up and even the rats having a snooze, after their Sunday devotions some ploughman lad and his bit of a lass would

27

sneak into the barn and hold their play and give each other a bit cuddle, frightened and glad and daft about it: and if maybe they thought they saw now and then some bogey or fairley peep out at them there was none to say that the thing wasn't likely Pict ghosts or the ghosts of the men long before peeping from the chill of that other land where flesh isn't warm nor kisses strong nor hands so sweet that they make you weep, nor terror now wonder their portion again, only a faint dim mist of remembering.

II

Now the nearest farm to Maiden Castle was the Mains of Balhaggarty along the coast, you went by a twisty winding path, leftwards the rocks and the sea and death if you weren't chancy and minding your feet, right the slope of the long flat fields that went careering west to the hills to the cup of the Howe, and, bright in Spring, the shape of Auchindreich's meikle hill. The Patons had been in Bahaggarty a bare twelve years and had done right well though they were half-gentry, old Paton an elder, precentor, he stood up of Sabbath in the old Free Kirk and intoned the hymns with a bit of a cough, like a turkey with a chunk of grain in its throat, and syne would burst into the Hundreth Psalm, all the choir following, low and genteel, and his wife, Mistress Paton, looking at him admiring, she thought there was no one like Sam in the world.

Folk said that was maybe as well for the world, Paton was as mean as he well could be, he'd four men fee'd, a cattler and three ploughmen, and paid them their silver each six month with a groan as though he were having a tooth dug out. But he farmed the land well in a skimpy way, with little manure and less of new seed, just holding the balance and skimming the land, ready for the time when he might leave and set himself up in a bigger place. He'd had two sons, or rather his wife, you'd have thought by Paton's holy-like look his mistress had maybe had them on her

28

own, the elder would never have been so indecent as take a part in such blushful work. The one of them, William, was a fine big lad, a seven years old and sturdy and strong, with a fine clear eye that you liked, he'd laugh, "'Lo, man, Losh you've got a funny face." And maybe then you wouldn't like him so much, queer how fond we all are of our faces. But he was cheery young soul for all that, aye into mischief out in the court, or creeping into the ploughmen's bothies and hearkening to the coarse songs they'd sing, about young ploughmen who slept with their masters' daughters and such like fairlies, all dirt and lies, a farmer's daughter never dreamed of sleeping with a ploughman unless she'd first had a look at his bank-book.

The second son Peter, a six years old, you didn't much like the look of, faith dark and young and calm with an impudent leer, not fine and excited when you patted his head but looking at you calm and cool, and you'd feel a bit of a fool in the act. But you never could abide those black-like folk, maybe they'd the blood of the Romans in them or some such coarse brood from ayont the sea. The wife, Mistress Paton, was an Aberdeen creature, she couldn't help that nor her funny speak, she called *buits beets* and *speens* for *spoons*, they were awfully ignorant folk in Aberdeen.

Well, that was the Mains of Balhaggarty, and outbye from it on the landward side lay the little two-horse farm of Moss Bank, farmed by a creature, Cruickshank the name, that was fairly a good farmer and an honest-like neighbour except when his temper got the better of him. He was small and compact and ground out in steel, blue, it showed in his half-shaved face, with a narrow jaw like a lantern, bashed, bits of eyes like chunks of ice, he'd stroke his cheeks when you asked his help, at harvest, maybe or off to the moors for a load of peats, and come striding along by your side to help, and swink at the work till the sun went down and the moon came up and your own hands were nearly dropping from their dripping wrist-bones. And if your horse might tread on his toes with a weight enough to send a ordinary man crack and make him kick the beast in the belly, he'd just give a cough and push it away, and get on with his chave, right canty and douce. And at last, when the lot of the work was done he'd nod goodbye, not wait for a dram, and as he moved off call back to know if you'd want his help the morn's morning?

You'd think "Well, of all the fine childes ever littered give me the Cruickshank billy, then" and maybe plan to take a bit rise out of him and get him neighbour-like, for more work. But sure as God in a day or so some ill-like thing would have happened between you, a couple of your hens would have ta'en a bit stroll through the dykes to his parks and picked a couple of fugitive grains and laid an egg as return, genteel, and turned about to come away home. And Cruickshank would have seen them, sure as death, given chase and caught them, and a bird in each hand stood cursing you and the universe blue, might you rot in hell on a hill of dead lice, you foul coarse nasty man-robber, you. And just as the air was turning a purple and the sun going down in a thunderstorm and all the folk within two miles coming tearing out of their houses to listen, he'd a voice like a foghorn, only not so sweet, had Cruickshank, he'd turn and go striding back to his steading, a hen in each hand, with a soulful squawk, and clump through the oozing sharn of the court, heavy-standing, deep-breathing his bull would be there with a shimmer and glimmer of eyes in the dark. So into the house and brush past his wife and cry "Hey, bring me a pen and some paper." His wife, a meikle great-jawed besom, nearly as big and ugly as Cruickshank, and of much the same temper, would snap back "Why?" And he'd say "My land's being ruined and lost with the dirt that let loose their beasts on me. Me! By the living God I'll learn the dirt — hey, where's that paper?" And that paper in hand he'd sit and write you a letter that would frizzle you up, telling you he held your hens, and you'd get them back when you came for them yourself and paid the damage that the brutes had made. And for near a six months or so after that when he met you at kirk or mart, on the turnpike, he'd pass with a face like an ill-ta'en coulter. There was no manners or flim-flams about Cruickshank at all, and sometimes you'd think there was damn little sense.

They'd had two sons, both grown up, the one Sandy bade at home with his father and ran a kind of Smithy at Moss Bank, coulters and pointers and the like he could manage, not much more, the creature half-daft, with a long loose mouth aye dribbling wet, and a dull and wavering eye in his head like a steer that's got water on the brain. He'd work for old Cruickshank with a good enough will a ten or eleven months of the year and then it would come on him all of a sudden, maybe shoeing a horse or eating his porridge or going out to the whins to ease himself, that something was queer and put out in his world, and you'd hear him give a roar like the bull and off he'd stride, clad or half-clad, and Moss Bank mightn't see him for a month or six weeks, the coarse brute would booze his way away south and join up with drivers off to the marts, and vanish away on the road to Edinburgh, and fight and steal and boast like a tink. And then one night he'd come sneaking back and chap at the door and come drooling in, and the father and mother would look at him grim and syne at each, other, and not say a word, real religious the two of them except when cursing the Lord Himself for afflicting decent honest folk that had never done Him any harm with a fool of a son like this daftie, Sandy and a wild and godless brute like Joe.

Now Joe had been settled in Aberdeen in a right fine job with a jeweller there and was getting on fine till the women got him, next thing there came a note to Mossbank that Joe would be put in the hands of the police unless his thefts were paid to the hilt. Old Cruickshank near brought a cloud-burst on the Mearns when he read that news, then yelled to his mistress to bring him his lum-hat and his good black suit. And into the two of them he got like mad, and went striding away down the road to Stonehaven, and boarded a train, into Aberdeen, the jeweller said he was very sorry, what else could he do, Joe was upstairs, and the sum was twenty five pounds if you please. And old Cruickshank paid it down like a lamb, if you can imagine a lamb like a leopard, and went up the stairs and howked out Joe and hauled him down and kicked his dowp out of the jeweller's shop. "Let me never look on your face again, you that's disgraced an honest man."

Joe was blubbering and sniftering like a seal by then, "But where am I going to go now, Father" and old Cruickshank said to him shortly, "To hell," and turned and made for the Aberdeen station.

Well, he went there, or nearly, it was just as bad, he joined the army, the Gordon Highlanders, full up of thieves and ill-doing men, grocers that had stolen cheese from their masters and childes that had got a lass with a bairn and run off to get-out of the paying for't, drunken ministers, schoolmasters that had done the kind of thing to this or that scholar that you didn't mention — and faith, he must fairly have felt at home. So off he went to the foreign parts, India and Africa and God knew where, sometimes he'd write a bit note to his mother, telling her how well he was getting on; and Cruickshank would give the note a glare "Don't show the foul tink's coarse scrawls to me. Him that can hardly spell his own name, and well brought up in a house like this."

For Cruickshank was an awful Liberal man, keen to support this creature Gladstone, he'd once travelled down to Edinburgh to hear him and come back more glinting and blue than ever, hating Tories worse than dirt, and the Reverend James Dallas worse than manure. Now, the Reverend James Dallas was the Auld Kirk minister, the kirk stood close in by the furthest of the Mossbank fields, huddling there in its bouroch of trees, dark firs, underneath were shady walks with the crunch of pine cones pringling and cool in the long heats of summer and in winter time a shady walk where the sparrows pecked. Within the trees lay kirk and manse, the kirk an old ramshackle place, high in the roof and narrow in the body, the Reverend James when he spoke from the pulpit looked so high in that narrow place you'd half think sometimes when the spirit was upon him he'd dive head first down on your lap. And all the ploughmen away at the back would grunt and shuffle their feet, not decent, and the Reverend James would look at them, bitter, and halt in the seventeenth point in his sermon till the kirk grew still and quiet as the grave, you'd hear the drone of a bumble bee and the splash of a bead of sweat from your nose as it tumbled into a body's beard. Then he'd start again on Hell and Heaven, more the former than the latter for sure, and speak of those who came to the Lord's House without reverence, ah, what would there last reward be in the hands of GED? For the Lord our Ged was a jealous Ged an the Kirk of Scotland a jealous kirk.

You thought that was maybe true enough, but it wasn't half so jealous as the Reverend himself, he'd a bonny young wife new come to the Manse, red-haired and young with a caller laugh, a schoolteacher lass that he'd met in Edinburgh when he was attending the Annual Assembly; and he'd met her at the house of her father, a minister, and fairly taken a fancy to her. So they'd wedded and the Reverend had brought her home, the congregation raised a subscription and had a bit concert for the presentation and the first elder, Paton, unveiled the thing, and there it was, a brave-like clock, in shape like a kirk with hands over the doors and scrolls all about and turrets and walls and the Lord knew what, a bargain piece. And the Reverend James look a look at it, bitter, and said that he thanked his people, he knew the value of time himself as the constant reminder of the purpose of Ged; and he hoped that those that presented it had thought of time in eternity. And some folk that had paid their shillings for the subscription went off from the concert saying to themselves that they'd thought of that, he needn't have feared, and they hoped that he would burn in it.

If he did folk said he would manage that all right if only he'd his wife well under his eye. For he followed her about like a calf a cow, he could hardly bear to let her out of his sight though while she was in it he paid little attention, cold and glum as a barn-door. She'd laugh and go whistling down through the pines, him pacing beside her, hands at his back, with a jealous look at the cones, at the hens, at the ploughmen turning their teams outbye, at Ged himself in the sky, you half-thought, that any should look at his mistress but him.

Well, that was the Reverend James Dallas, then, and his jealousy swished across the Howe and fixed on the other kirk of the parish, the wee Free Kirk that stood by the turnpike, a new-like place of a daft red stone, without a steeple and it hadn't a choir, more like a byre with its dickie on, than a kirk at all, said Camlin of Badymicks. The most of the folk that squatted in it, were the shopkeeper creatures that came from the Howe villages and the smithies around and joineries. The kind of dirt that doubted the gentry and think they know better than the Lord Himself. The only farmer in its congregation was Cruickshank of Mossbank sitting close up under the lithe of the pulpit, his arms crossed and his eye fixed stern on the face of the Reverend Adam Smith, shining above him in the Free Kirk pulpit like a sun seen through a maiden fog.

The Reverend Adam was surely the queerest billy that ever had graced a pulpit, in faith. He wasn't much of a preacher, dreich, with a long slow voice that sent you to sleep, hardly a mention of heaven or hell or the burning that waited on all your neighbours, and he wasn't strong on infant damnation and hardly ever mentioned Elijah. Free Kirk folk being what they are, a set of ramshackle radical loons that would believe nearly anything they heard if only it hadn't been heard before, could stick such preaching and not be aggrieved, especially if the minister was a fine-like creature outside the kirk and its holy mumble, newsy and genial and stopping for a gossip, coming striding in to sit by the fire and drink a bowl of sour milk with the mistress. But the Reverend Adam neither preached nor peregrinated, your old mother would be lying at the edge of death and say

34

"Will you get the minister for me? There's a wee bit thing that I'd like explained in the doctrine of everlasting damnation; forbye, he might put up a bit of a prayer." And off you'd go in search of the creature, and knock at his door and the housekeeper come, and she'd shake her head, he was awful busy. You'd say "Oh? Is he? Well, my mother's dying," and at last be led to the Reverend's study, a hotter and hotch of the queerest dirt, birds in cages and birds on rails, and old eggs and bits of flints and swords and charts and measurements, a telescope, and an awful skeleton inside a glass press that made your fairly grue to look on. And the Reverend would turn round his big fat face and peer at you from his wee twink eyes, you'd tell what you needed and he'd grunt "Very well" and his eyes grow dreamy and far away and start on his scribbling as before. And you'd wait till you couldn't abide it longer: "Minister, will you come with a prayer for my mother? She's sinking fast" and he'd start around "Sinking? What? A ship off the Howe" — the fool had forgotten that you were there.

And when at last he'd come with the prayer and you'd take him along to your mother's room and she'd ask him the point about burning forever, instead of soothing her off, just quiet, with some bit lie to soothe the old body and let her go to hell with an easy mind, he'd boom out that there were Three Points at least to look at in this subject, and start on the Early Fathers, what they'd said about it and argued about it, a rare lot of tinks those Fathers had been, what Kant had said, and a creature Spinoza, the views of the Brahmins and the Buddhists and Bulgarians, and what that foul creature Mohammed had thought, him that had a dozen women at his call and expected to have a million in heaven. And while he was arguing and getting interested your mother would slip from under his hands, and you'd pull at his sleeve. "Well, sir, that'll do. No doubt the old woman's now arguing the point with Kant and Mohammed in another place."

Faith, it was maybe more that and a chance, folk said, that the big-bellied brute was keen on Mohammed. What about him and that housekeeper of his, a decent-like woman with a face like a scone, but fair a bunk of a figure for all that. Did he and her aye keep a separate room, and if that was so why was there aye a light late in hers at night, never in his? And how was it the creature could wear those brave-like clothes that she did? And how was it, if it wasn't his conscience, faith, that the Reverend Adam was hardly ever at home? instead, away over Auchindreich Hill, measuring the Devil's Footstep there, or turning up boulders and old-time graves where the Picts and the like ill folk were buried in a way just as coarse as Burke & Hare.

East, landwards of the Free Kirk rose Auchindreich, spreading and winding back in the daylight, north along the road was the toun of the Howe, and south-east before you came to it two small crofts and a fair sized farm. Now the childe in the croft of Lamahip was a meikle great brute of a man called Gunn, long and lank with a great bald head and a long bald coulter of a red-edged nose, he farmed well and kept the place trig and his wife and three daughters in a decent-like way. And, faith, you'd have given him credit for that if it wasn't he was the greatest liar that ever was seen in the Howe or the Gowe. If he drove a steer to the mart in Stonehyve and sold it maybe for a nine or ten pounds, would that be a nine or ten pounds when he met you down in the pub at the end of the day? Not it, it would be a nineteen by then, and before the evening was out and the pub had closed it was maybe nearer twenty-nine; and he'd boast and blow all the way to the Howe, staggering from side to side of the road and sitting down every now and then to weep over the lasses he had long syne, the lasses had aye liked him well, you heard, and he'd once slept with a Lady in Tamintoul, she'd wanted him to marry her and work their estate, but he'd given it all up, the daft fool that he'd been, to take over the managership of a forest in Breadalbane — had you heard about that? And you'd say "God, aye, often," and haul him to his feet and off along the road again, up over the hill that climbs from

Stonehyve in the quietude of a long June night, you looking back on the whisper and gleam of Stonehaven, forward to the ruins of Dunnottar Castle, black and immense against the sky, the air filled with the clamour of seagulls wings as they pelted inland from a coming storm.

His wife was a thin little red-headed woman, canty and kind and maybe the best cook that ever yer had been seen in the district, she could bake oatcakes that would melt between your jaws as a thin rime of frost on the edge of a plough, baps that would make a man dream of heaven, not the one of the Reverend Dallas, and could cook that foul South dish the haggis in a way that made the damn thing nearly eatable, not as usual with a smell like a neglected midden and a taste to match, or so you imagined, not that you'd ever eaten middens. And she'd say as she put a fresh scone on the girdle "But they're not like the fine cakes you had from your Lady, are they now, Hugh," with a smile in her eye, and he'd answer up solemn, No, God, they weren't, but still and on, she did not so bad. And she'd smile at the fire, kneeling with the turning fork, small and compact, and keeping to herself, you couldn't but like the little creature.

Faith, that was more than the case with the daughters, the oldest, Jean, had a face like a sow, a holy-like sow that had taken to religion instead of to litters as would have been more seemly. But God knows there was no one fool enough in the Howe to offer to bed her and help in that though she'd seen only a twenty-three summers and would maybe have been all right to cuddle if you could have met her alone in the dark, when you couldn't see her face, you don't cuddle faces. But she never went out of a night, not her, instead sat at home and mended and sewed and read Good Works and was fair genteel, and if ever she heard a bit curse now and then from old Hugh Gunn or some lad dropped in to hear the latest or peek at her sister she'd raised up her eyes as though she suffered from wind and depress her jaws as though it was colic, fair entertaining a man as he watched.

But her sister Queen was a kittler bitch, dark and narrow with a fine long leg, black curly hair in ringlets about her and a pale quiet face but a blazing eye. She was a dress-maker and worked the most of the day above the shop down there in the Howe, sewing up the bit wives that wanted a dress on the cheap without the expense of going to Stonehyve, or needed their lasses trigged out for the kirk, or wanted the bands of their frocks let out when another bairn was found on the way. And Queen Gunn would sit and sew there all day and at night would sit and just read and read, books and books, birns of the dirt, not godly-like books or learned ones, but stories of viscounts and earls and the like and how the young heir was lost in the snow, and how bonny Prince Charlie had been so bonny — as from the name you had half-supposed. And in spite of her glower and that blaze in her eye she'd little or no time at all for the lads; and the Lord alone knew what she wanted, the creature.

Now the second of the crofts in that little bouroch was Badymicks that stood outbye the land of Cruickshank, a little low dirty skleiter of place, the biggings were old and tumbling down, propped up here and there with a tree or so, or a rickle of bricks or an old Devil Stone brought there by Arch Camlin from one of his walks. He was the only Camlin that had come in the Howe and faith, folk said that that was as well, one of the breed was more than enough, the Camlins were thicker in the Howe than fleas, farmers and croppers and crofters and horse-traders, horse-steal-ers, poachers and dairymen, and the Lord knew what, if a Camlin stole your watch at a fair and you cried on a bobby to stop the thief it was ten to one, in Fordoun or Laurence-kirk, the boby would be of one of the Camlins too, and run you in for slandering a relative. Well, Arch was maybe the best of the lot, a forty years or so old, swack and lithe, with a clean-shaven face and meikle dark eyes. He'd married a second time late in life, a creature from the way of Aber-deen, she'd come to Badymicks a gey canty dame, with fine fat buttocks and a fine fat smile, she'd been a maid to a couple of old women that had worn away through a slow slope of years as worms wear off from sight to a grave. They'd left her a couple of hundred pounds and just as she was wondering what to do with it along came Arch Camlin on some ploy or other and picked up the two hundred in his stride, so to speak, and the poor lass with them and carted the lot away to tumbledown Badymicks. And there for a while it had been well enough, Arch was land-mad, at it all day criss-crossing his ploughing with a sholt and a cow and planning the draining of the sodden fields, he could work the average man near to death. And coming from the fields to his supper at night he'd dally with the woman and give her a squeeze and she put on a fine dress and smile at him soft, and all had been well for a little time.

But Arch had been married long afore that, his first wife had died and left a wee lass, Rachel, that Arch had put out to suck with an old widow woman in a village of the Howe. So now Arch brought this quean Rachel home, short and dark with a sallow skin, black-haired, black-browed, with a bit of a limp, and her eyes wide with a kind of wonder, you couldn't make up your mind on the lass, but Mistress Camlin made up hers at once, she couldn't abide her and would hardly heed her, the little lass would follow Arch all day long out in the fields, in the flare of sun, in dripping rains on autumn's edge, keen and green on a morning in Spring you'd hear her cry him into meat. She was only five when she came to Badymicks and the next year the new family started to come, first a loon and then a lass, and there was every sign in this year as well that another bairn was hot on the way. And no sooner had the first put in its appearance that the gentility went from poor Jess. She grew whiny and complainy and bunched in the middle and seemed hardly to ken her head from her feet, and even if she did what to do with either, and she'd stare at Eda, Bogmuck's housekeeper, and shake her head and wonder aloud how any women could get pleasure out of *that*.

Bogmuck was the second biggest place in the parish, and the man that had ta' on it on the new thirteen years' lease was a well-set up and well-doing childe, Dalsack the name, from a bothy in Bogjorgan. He was maybe a forty, forty-five years old, with whiskers down the side of his face, decent, and aye wore a top-hat on Sundays, an elder at the kirk, and a fine, cheery soul. He made silver as some folk made dirt or bairns, Dalsack had had over much sense for the latter, he'd never married and never would, over shy to be taken in by any woman. He was a knowledgeable and skilly man, cheery-like and the best of neighbours if maybe a wee bit close with his silver. And why shouldn't he be? It was only dirt that brought themselves to paupers' graves that would fling good money about for nothing. Well, God, if that was the case, as they said, there was little chance of Dalsack a pauper, he'd smile, big and cheery but careful to the last bit farthing there was, as he paid out the two fee'd men of Bogmuck or the money the housekeeper wanted to pay for groceries and the like brought up from Bervie. For a good six years he'd had a housekeeper, a decent young woman though awful quiet, that did right well and never raised scandal, no fear of that with Dalsack about, he must nearly have fainted with shyness, you thought, when first he found himself in his mother's bed: in the bed of another woman, faith, he'd dissolve into nothing but one raddle of a blush.

So things were canty and quiet enough till the January of 1880 came in, and then the housekeeper left of a sudden, nobody got to the bottom of it, she packed her bag and went trudging away, folk saw her come past the houses of the village with her face white and set, could it be that she had the belly-ache? And one or two cried to her to come in and sit her down for a cup of tea — was she off to Stonehyve then, would it be? But she just shook her head and went trudging on and that was the last of her seen in the Howe.

And faith, Dalsack didn't meet her marrow. Instead, he fee'd to Bogmuck a quean whose capers were known all over the Howe, Eda Lyell, a shameless limmer, she came from Drumlithie, a bonny like quean, but already with three bairns on her hands and each of them by a different

40

father. Folk shook their heads when they heard of her coming and the Reverend Dallas went to Dalsack and told him bitter that the parish would be tainted and riven with sin if he brought this woman to Bogmuck, a foul insult in the face of Ged. But Dalsack just gave his nose a stroke and smiled and said canny that he didn't think so. And come she did in a week or less, trailing over the head of Auchindreich hill with her three weans clinging on to her skirts, half-dead with the voyage through the whins and broom; and the whole of the village made a leap for its windows and stared at her as she panted by, the foul trollop that she was, said all the women, and the men gave a bit of a lick at their lips, well, well, fine buttocks and a fine like back.

But she'd more than that, some thought it clean shameful, for before she had been a three months in the Howe Eda was a favourite with every soul, big and strapping with a flushed, bonny face and hair like corn, ripe corn smoothed out in flat waves in sun under the ripple of a harvest guff, and a laugh that was deep and clear and snell, snell and sweet as a wind at night. There wasn't a more helpful body in the Howe, or more obliging, she worked like a nigger indoors and out — ay, Dalsack had fairly a bargain in her. Near the only creature that still looked down on her was the Reverend James Dallas, as you may well have guessed, he met her out in the parks one day, her spreading dung under the coming of April, a white-like morning, dew about, and the peewits wailing and crying like mad. And he said to her "Are you the woman of Badymicks," and she nodded to him blithe, "Ay, sir, I am that." "Then see there are no more fatherless bairns brought into the world by you to your shame. Give you good-day" and he went striding off, leaving Eda staring after him, big and tall and sonsy and flushed, frozen a minute, a ploughman was by and heard every word and told the tale. And when folk had heard they said it was shameful, who was he to slander the poor quean like that? Maybe he was mad that for all his trying and the guarding of that Edinburgh wife of his he couldn't bring a single bairn in the world, let alone a healthy bit three like Eda's.

Now the village was hardly a village at all, long lines of houses fronting the road and across that the tumbling parks of the farms and the crofts, the rigs of Badymicks, the curving whin lands seeping to Bogmuck, beyond that far and a two miles off the sea and the high roofs of Maiden Castle. One end of the village was the school and schoolhouse where old Dominie Moncrief lived with his daughter, him an old creature near to retiring, her a braw lass awful keen on the lads. Betwixt was the line of the cottar's houses for roadmen and folk of like ilk and bang at the other end of the line the village shop and post-office in one, a fine big place where you'd buy anything, tow and tea and marmalade, and gigham strips and crinolines and baps and bags of peasmeal and rice and hooks and eyes and needles and stays, boots for the bairns for going to the kirk, and anything from a flea to a granite gravestone. The Munros were the folk that ran the place, father and son, and old Munro, that was Alick, was fair dottled by then and mixing up time and space and all, he'd come peering behind a bale to serve you, his runkled old face in the light of the crusie looking like one of the salted fish the shop sold in such stores for the winter's dinner. He aye wore a nightcap upon his head and fingerless mittens on his hands, poor stock, and he it was the postmaster, Johnnie his son carried round the letters. Folk had made a bit rhyme about old Munro —

He wears a nightcap on his head
And muggins on his han'
And every soul that sees him pass
Cries Mighty, what a man!

But he'd never heard that, the thrawn old tyke, and thought himself right well respected, and would read any letter that came to you all over from back to front of the envelope with a sharp like look as much as to say "And who are you to be having letters and disturbing a man at his real work, then?" So he knew all the things that were going on, some said that he and his son, young Johnnie, steamed open every letter there was, God knows they got little for their pains if they did.

Young Johnnie was a bit of a cripple, like, thin and souple, but his right leg twisted on back to front as though he'd made up his mind to go back and never come into the world at all. But faith, Mistress Munro had beaten him at that, out into the world he'd come at last, a thirty years before that time, and his mother had taken a look at him and then turned her face and just passed away. And Munro was once telling that tale in the shop and a ploughman childe said he didn't wonder, it was the kind of face to turn even a mother. And Johnnie the cripple foamed with rage and went about swearing for days what he'd have done if that ploughman had stayed — he was awful for thinking himself a terror, poor Johnnie.

Well, whether or no it was true that they steamed the letters it was from the post office that the news spread round, a two months before the Lammas came in, that the Stratouns were coming back to the Howe, to Maiden Castle down by the sea that had lain lost and empty ten years. John Stratoun the son was coming back, he'd a wife and three bairns and was coming from Montrose to farm the land and put it to right and establish the Stratouns on the land again.

THE STRATOUNS

I

Alick was eight and Peter five and Keith just turned a three years old the spring when John Stratoun left Montrose and carted the family and gear he had to Maiden Castle. He'd been foreman for the contractor in the new drains they were laying in Montrose, had father, he'd been doing that kind of work for years, but never much satisfied, he thought little of towns; and never he could take a walk on a Sabbath outside the town through the greening parks but that he would stop and dawdle and peer down at the earth and test the corn-heads and nod his own head at the nodding corn, "Aye, God, but it's canty stuff to look at."

Mother would say in her sharp-like way "Don't swear like that in front of the little 'uns" and father would say "Od, lass, did I swear? Well, well, they would hardly know what I meant" and give Alick's hair a bit of a tug, or make out he was thrappling Peter's long throat; but you were only a baby then, Keith, and he'd pitch you up in the air, high, suddenly the fields rose high, you saw Montrose and the gleam of the sea, flat and pale, and gave a scream, not frightened, you liked it, just couldn't help the scream. Mother would give another snort, such awful conduct on a Sabbath, this, what ever would the neighbours say if they saw?

Well, the stay in Montrose came suddenly to an end, Granny that bade at the other end of the town, in a little house like a lop-eared hare, died at last at her kitchen table one day, with a meikle bowl of brose before her and a coarse-like book spread out on her lap. She'd fair been a right fine granny, Keith thought, she never come into the house but she brought a man sticks of candy to suck right to the end and make himself sick, but Mother you thought didn't like her much, you'd heard her say to father once that of all the coarse creatures she'd ever set eyes on his

44

mother, she thought, was nearly the worst.

Father had just said in his quiet-like way, "'Od, lass, and maybe you're right, 'od, aye" and mother had looked mad enough to burst, if there was a thing that she couldn't abide worse than somebody to argue with her it was somebody who gave in all the time. And she'd skelped Alick's ear for leaning over the fire, and swooshed Peter out of her way from the table, and no doubt would have given you a shake as well if it hadn't been you were sitting good as gold, in a corner, cuddling the big cat, Tibbie. "Right? Ay, I'm right. And a bonny look out to think that such blood runs in the little 'uns." You wondered what kind of blood it was, Granny's, you thought it blue, not black, her hands were white and skinny and thin and you could see the veins when they lay at rest; maybe Mother thought blue blood awful coarse.

Well, Granny died and all the house in Montrose was fair in a stew for a day or so, mother coming and going and weeping now and then, loud out she wept, just like yourself, "Oh, it's awful, awful, poor creature, poor creature," she meant Granny, and father patted her shoulder "Wheesht, lass, wheesht, she's safe and at rest." But Mother just wept a bit more at that, and Alick that was making a face behind her, making on he was weeping as well, real daft, was so funny that you and Peter burst out in a laugh. And at that Mother stopped from her greeting at once and wheeled round and smacked Alick one on the ear, and you and Peter got a bit of a shake. "Think shame of yourselves, you coarse little brutes. Laughing and your granny new in her grave. Whatever would the neighbours say if they heard?" And father said quiet and bit wearied-like "Och, they'd just say it was Granny's coarse blood."

But syne Father found he'd been left nearly three hundred pounds, he'd never suspected, neither had Mother, that Granny had nearly as much as that, and they sat up half the night whispering about it, Mother loud out saying "Yea" and "Nay", father in a canny whisper, low, so that you and Peter and Alick wouldn't waken in the meikle box bed ayont the fire — you were all three awake and hearing each word and tickling each other under the sheets. And whenever father might raise his voice a wee, Mother would whisper fierce "Wheesht! You'll waken the bairns, man" herself loud enough to waken the dead.

And what they were arguing and bargying about was whether or not to leave Montrose and trail away up through the Howe to some place that father called Maiden Castle. Mother was just as keen as father, but she wouldn't let on to that, not her, she'd to be prigged and pleaded with half that night and most of the next day, and again next night till at last father said with a bit of a sigh "All right, lass. Then we'll stay where we are."

At that Mother flared up "Stay here in a toun when you've a fine farm away in the Howe? Have you no spunk at all to try and make you improve yourself?" and father said nothing, just smoked his pipe, and mother started singing a hymn-tune, loud, she aye did that when blazing with rage; so you knew that father had won the battle.

II

Father was a meikle big man with a beard, or so you aye thought, but Alick didn't, he said the old man wasn't bad, but only a wee chap, and couldn't fight a bobby. But father had fought worse than bobbies in his time, when Granny came down to live in Montrose he'd gone to school and grown tired of that and then worked in a flax-mill and tired of that, till Granny had asked him in the name of God what did he think there was to turn his useless hands to, then? And father had said "The land" and Granny had said that was daft, he couldn't be a ploughman, the Stratouns had a name to keep up in the Howe. So father had borrowed some money from her and emigrated to a place called America, awful wild and full up of buffaloes and bears and wolves that at night came snuffling under the doors of the sheds where father and others slept, snuffle, snuffle in the moonlight. If they peered through the cracks they'd see the glare of the eyes below. But father said he hadn't been feared when he'd tell you the stories, and you knew he hadn't, he'd just thought "Ay, losh, but the poor beasts are famished" and turned over to sleep in the other side. There was an awful queer lot of men there, Germans and Poles and such-like folk, father hardly knew a word they said, that wouldn't have scunnered him, the farming did. For it wasn't real farming at all, he told, just miles and miles of sweet damn all, prairie and long grass and holes in the horizon, and a bleak, dull sky night and day, hardly a tree and at night a moon so big and red it seemed to a man the damn thing would come banging down on the earth. And the ploughs were the queerest and daftest things, the cattle were scrawny and ill-kept beasts; and after six years John Stratoun looked about and decided he'd just have a look at Scotland. And off he set and home he had come, in a cattle-boat, with ninety pounds of his savings tied up in a little pock under his arm-pit, awful safe, but when he got into Glasgow he'd forgot to keep out any change and nearly had to take all his clothes off in the railway station to pay for his ticket.

Well, he got back to Montrose, still the same, the feuch of it he smelt from the railway carriage, he'd never much liked the place, you knew, though father had a good word for near everything, every place, every soul, he ever had known, he'd have said that the devil wasn't maybe so bad, it was just the climate of hell that tried him. But as the train came coasting the sea and Montrose was below father looked out, it was harvest time, they were cutting the fields, a long line of scythemen and gatherers behind, and one of the gatherers straightened up and looked at the train and father at her, and it was mother, though she didn't know it, father did, he made up his mind at that minute, he would say, that she was to be mother (and Alick in bed would snigger about that, and say funny things and you couldn't but laugh).

She wasn't much taller than father was, but well-made, a fine-covered woman with flaming red hair and sharp blue eyes and full red lips and white strong teeth; and father thought her the bonniest thing he'd seen in all the days of his life. And he'd hardly got into Montrose with his things and knocked up Granny, she'd said "Oh, it's you? Shut the door John, I can't abide draughts" than he was out of the place again, and bapping away back by the railway track through the long haycocks that posed to the sun and over soft stubble and so to that park.

And he made himself acquaint at the place, and got a fee there and wedded mother. And they finished the feeing and came into Montrose, to work at contracting, and that father stuck till Granny was carried at last to her grave, she's a stone above it; and years after that Keith once had a spare hour on his hands, autumn, dripping with rain and a sough of the soft and slimy sea wind from the sea of Montrose was a scum on the roofs, and he wandered into the graveyard, dark, and looked for that stone and found it and read, queer and moved:

Ann Stratoun.
Aged 89.
"And still he giveth his beloved sleep."

III

It was late in the jog of an April day when our flitting of Montrose came through the Howe, over the hill of Auchindreich and into the crinkly cup of the village, shining weather, far up all day as we came rode little clouds like lost feathers, high, as though some bird were lost in the lift, moulting maybe, and beyond it the sun, and clear and sharp all about the roads the tang and whiff of the sun-touched earth, warm and stirring, little mists riding them by the Luther bridge, and the teeth of a rainbow came out and rode the seaward hills by Johnston Tower. I couldn't see it though Alick held me up and pointed it out from the

48

back box-cart. And then I was sleeping to the chug and sway of the horses' hooves and the moving cart and on the three carts rumbled along together, father sitting in the lead, behind him the gear he'd gotten for his farming and a dozen hens locked up in a coup, and two ploughs dismantled and loaded up and high towering about it all the bit of the furniture that wouldn't go into the second cart, a great oak wardrobe from Maiden Castle carted away from there thirty five years before when Granny moved from the place to Montrose.

And there was Laurencekirk all asleep, with its lint-mills and its meikle bobbies about, with their big straw hats and their long-falling beards. Now and then we met in with some creature traipsing along the turnpike, a tink with bare feet and hardly a stitch, his rotten sark sticking out from his breeks, behind him his wife with a birn of bairns, they'd cry out for silver and father would nod "'Od, aye we can surely spare you a something." Mother was mad and said it was wastery, what would tinks like that do with your bawbees that you'd earned yourself by the sweat of your brow? Spend it on drink, the foul stinking creatures. And Father said agreeably "Oh ay, no doubt" giving his long brown beard a bit wipe, his brown eyes, mild, lifted up to the hills, his hands soft on the reins of the new mare, Bess.

Alick came behind with the second cart, awful proud and sitting up there like a monkey, chirking away at the gelding, Sam, Sam paying no heed but flinging his legs fine and sonsy and switching his tail and stopping now and then to ease himself, the tail switched up in Alick's face. The furniture and gear was piled in that cart and the meat we'd need when we'd gotten to Maiden, and all our clothes and the like of things, Mother as well, sitting up genteel, dressed in best black and her eyes all about, sharp and clear on everything, only her hair was just like a flame that didn't seem somehow to go with the eyes, said Geordie Allison, our new fee'd man. And he said Ay, God, she no doubt led old Stratoun a dance and fairly believed that she wore the breeks.

Geordie Allison himself drove the last of the carts, a well set-up and stocky man with a long moustache and a long red neck, he'd worked for father once in Montrose though he was a ploughman and like father couldn't stick a job that wasn't out on the land. He was awful old, we all of us thought, maybe thirty or forty or nearly a hundred, Mother didn't like him much, we were sure, she'd been awful shocked by the way he spoke to the minister man outbye from Mondynes.

We'd newly come through the wee toun of Fordoun when we met the minister, out for a walk, with his black flat hat and his long black clothes, he stood to the side of the road, and father lifted his hat to him and mother bobbed, as folk had to do when they met in with a minister childe. The minister held up his hand and father hauled at the head of Bess and the whole three carts came showding to a halt while the minister ran his eyes over us all, wee pig eyes and not very bonny, and asked where we were going, where we'd come from, what were our ages, were we godly folk. And father just sat and looked at him douce, but mother bridled and answered him short, and at last Geordie Allison cried out from the back "Are we standing all day with this havering skate? If he's no place to sleep let him take to the ditch, we've to get to Maiden afore the sun sets."

Mother had been awful ashamed and red, she said after that she was black affronted, whatever would the minister say about them? them that had aye been decent folk. But father just chirked to make Bess get up "Ay, no doubt he'll have a bit tale to tell, the lad had a nasty look in his eye. But ministers aye are creatures like that, they've nothing to do but stand and claik." And Mother said wheesht, not to talk that way and her trying to bring up the bairns God-fearing. And Geordie Allison muttered at the back there was surely a difference between fearing God and fearing the claik of a flat-faced goat with a flat bottom bulging out his black breeks.

Then we came to a ridge between the hills, early after-noon, Peter only asleep, snoozing dead to the world, so

50

tired, on the shelvin lashed to the back of the cart. And father said "Well, we'll stop a while here and have a bit feed," and Mother said no, she wouldn't have folk think they were tinks, they could eat a piece as they went along. But father just gave his brown beard a stroke and led the carts in by the side of the road, a burn flowed and spun and loitered below, minnows were flicking gold in the shadows, far up over Geyriesmuir hill there were peewits crying and crying, crying, the sound woke Peter and he cried as well, lost and amazed a minute, in the midst of the bright, clean, shining land where only far off in other parks were the moving specks of men at the harrows. And Mother came running and lifted him down and nursed him and said that he was her dawtie, he didn't much like it, Alick was sneering "Aye, mammy's pet" and I was grinning, he could sleep his head into train oil, Peter.

But Geordie Allison was out and about, gathering broom roots and hackles of whins, and coming striding back for the kettle and tearing off down to the burn with it and setting it loaded over the fire, tea hot steaming in a mighty short while, all sitting around to drink from the cups, and eat the fine oatcakes. Mother could make better oatcakes and scones than any other soul in the Howe, or so she was to think till she got to the village and heard of the reputation of Mrs Gunn. We'd brought a great kebbuck of cheese as well, old and dried, full of caraway seeds and with long blue streaks out and in, all crumbly, and we all ate hearty, father sitting by mother and as he finished he gave her a smack on the bottom as she stood to pour him another cup "Faith, creature, you can fair make a tasty meal, even though it's only by the side of a road."

Mother said "Keep your hands to yourself and don't haver. What would folk say if they saw you, eh?"

"'Od, they'd go blue at the gills with envy. Let them see, let them see. Well, Keith my man, what do you think of the Upper Howe?"

But you just yawned and were sleepy again and a little bit frightened of the horses, the place, the clear cold crying of the long grey birds, all this business of going to a farm where Alick said there would be great big bulls to gore you to death, and swine that ate men, a swine had once eaten a man in Montrose, and maybe lions and wolves and bears, in an awful old Castle full of ghosts and golochs and awful things. But you chirped up "Fine, faither" and he said you were a gey bit lad, a man before your mother all right, and then as your face grew all red and flushed he rose and carried you away from the rest, round the corner behind the whins. Other men didn't do that kind of thing, but father did, he hadn't any shame. Mother said it sometimes left her just black affronted the womanish things he could turn to. But you liked it, you gripped his hand coming back, and he patted your head, his eyes far way, forward and upward to the cup of the Howe.

And the horses were bitted and the cart-stands let down and father and Geordie lighted their pipes, blue puff-puffs, and mother smoothed down her dress, looking this way and that, with sharp, quick eyes, in case a neighbour might be looking on, though there wasn't one within twenty miles. And you all piled into the carts again and went on through the long spring afternoon, hardly it seemed it would ever end, down past Drimlithie, white and cold and sleeping under the Trusta hills, here the Grampians came marching down, green-brown, towering in snow far in the peaks, beyond as you turned by the farm of Kandy, far up and across through rising slopes, rose Auchindreich all dark and wild with the winding white track that climbed by Barras to the end of our road.

Bunches of firs in long flat plantations, the road all sossed where they grew each side, and then you were through the Fiddes woods and turned up right to tackle the hill, the sun going down and greyness coming over the hard, clear afternoon. Mother got down from the second cart and came and wrapped up the bairns, tight, in plaids, they could hardly move, Peter didn't care, just snored on, he snored with his mouth wide open and you would sometimes watch the waggle of a thing inside like a little red frog, to and fro, and think what an awful thing was a mouth, you'd queer-like fancies even then.

And looking out from the plodding carts as the last of the little farms passed you saw the dark was following you along the road and between the whins, like a creeping panther or a long black wolf, pad-pad in long loping shadow play, what if the thing were to catch you here? And as you thought that it rushed and caught, the carts were in darkness, slow thump, thump, hares were running and scuttling across the deeps of the road and far away, miles off in some lithe sheltered peak a cow was mooing in the evening quiet. Then lights began to prink here and there as they rose and rose, to the roof of the world as it seemed, though only the lip of the Howe, up and up to the long flat ridge where in ancient times the long-dead heathen had built their circles and worshipped their gods, died, passed, been children, been bairns and dreamed and watched long wolf-shapes slipper and slide about their habitations in dark, unfriended, unguarded by such a one as Geordie Allison with a fine long whip and a fine long tongue; he wasn't frightened at anything, Geordie, the dark or a horse or even Mother.

You went rumbling through the Howe in the dark, father striding ahead with a lantern, mother following leading Bess. Bess hungry and dribbling soft at her hand, Mother saying "Feuch, you nasty brute" as the mare wetted her fine Sabbath gloves; and then was sorry in the way she would be, "Poor lass, are you wearied for your stable, then?" At that Bess nibbled some more and snickered, then shoved down her head and went bapping on, no meat till the end of the road, she knew.

Father hadn't been down that road since nearly a thirty five years, last time running and sobbing up this brae, past Badymicks to the village to send for a doctor to come look at his father dead and spread out by the barn of Maiden. But he hadn't forgotten it, striding ahead, the lantern gripped sure and canny in his hand, no fairlies vexed him minding that last time, there was nothing from the other world ever vexed a decent man if he minded his own business and hurt no one, he would face up to God at the Judgment Day, Father, and knock the shag from his pipe; "Ay, Lord, this is fairly a braw place you have," kind and undisturbed and sure as ever, sometimes there was something in that surety of his that half-frightened Mother, was there ever such a man? And she'd cease to scold him and fuss around, seeing to his boots or his breeks or his meat, and creep against him, alone at night, and his arm go round her corded and strong "Well, lass, tired lass?" Oh — a fine lad, John, but she mustn't be a daft, soft fool and think that.

And Mother gave Bess's reins a tug, Bess heeded nothing, swinging along, past Badymicks and the smells of Bogmuck. Father sniffed at the smells of the midden, ay, they'd fairly a fine collection of guffs, fine for the crops, fine for the crops. And already he was half-impatient to be home and settled in and get on with the work — God, man, what a smell was dung at night thick and spread on the waiting land!

But now a new smell was meeting the carts, sharp and tart and salt in the throat, the smell of the sea, and then its sound, a cry and whisper down in the dark as you wound by an over-grown rutted lane, a weasel came out and spat at Father and once the long shape of some sheep-killing dog snarled at him from the lithe of a hedge, but he paid no heed, going cannily on. He'd fallen to a wheeber, soft and quiet, a song he'd often sing to the lads:

> "Oh, it's hame, dearie, hame, fain
>   wad I be,
> Hame, dearie, hame, in my ain
>   countree,
> There's a gleam upon the bird
>   and there's blossom on the tree,
> And I'm wearin' hame
>   to my ain countree."

And suddenly, great and gaunt, owl-haunted, Maiden Castle.

The boys were never to forget that spring, it wove into the fabric of their beings and spread scent and smell and taste and sound, till it obscured into a faint far mist all their days and nights in the town of Montrose. And it seemed they had bidden at Maiden forever, and would surely bide there forever. Alick would say By God he hoped not, he would rather bide in a midden, he would.

The three loons slept in the meikle box bed set up in the kitchen of the windy Castle, so long and wide with its clay floor and its low wood beams, all black and caked, that at night when you looked out from the blankets it seemed you slept in the middle of a park, far off across its stretching rigs the fire gleamed low by the meikle lum, the grandfather clock by the little low window was another door and the moonlight crept and veered and flowed on the ground, nearer and nearer, you could hear it come. And above that sound, unending, unbegun, the pelt of the tide down under Maiden, soft and whispering, where dead men were, fishes, and great big ugsome beasts, without feet or faces, like giant snails, they crept out at night from the caves in the rocks and came sniffling, sniffling up the rocks, sniffling and rolling, they'd get in at the window, you could hear the slime-scrape of a beast on the walls. And you'd bury your head below the bed-clothes and cuddle close to the sleeping Peter, he in the middle, Alick far at the side. You were only little and had to lie in the front, no defence. And Peter would stop in his snoring a minute and consider, and give a grunt and a torn groan, and start in hard at his snoring again till you'd think in a minute his head would fall off, clean sawn through — Losh, how he could sleep!

And at last so would you, curled up and small, and the next thing you know that the morning was come, five o'clock and father and mother up, a windy dawn on the edge of the dark, the dark rolling back from the sleeping Howe parks like a tide of ink, a keen Spring wind breenging and spitting in from the sea, gulls on its tail — ay, rain to-day. And Father would button up his jacket and grab a great horn lantern in each hand, and cry up the stairs, "Are you ready, Geo man?" and Geordie Allison come clattering down and out they go to tend to the cattle, the horses, the pigs, tackitty boots striking fire from the stones in the close as they waded through the midden over to the dim sleeping cattle court, frosty in steam from the breath of the kine.

Behind in the kitchen Mother, a scarf wrapped round her flaming hair, would be shooting to and fro and back and about and up again, collecting pails and sieves and pans, and oilcake for the calves and a little dish to give the cats that bade in the byre, five of the brutes, a taste of milk. And at last, with a guano sack about her, as an apron, and her frock kilted up high, she'd go banging out of the kitchen door; and Alick would groan from the far side of the bed: "The old bitch would waken Kinneff Kirkyard," he was funny, Alick, aye fighting with Mother.

Father and Geordie would be meating the horses, four of them now, fat and neighing, waiting their corn and straw steamed with treacle, as Mother opened the door of the byre and went in to the hanging lantern there, and banged down her pails on the calsay floors. The cats would come tearing out to meet her, mewing and purring, and mother would say "Get out of my way, you orra dirt!" and kick them aside, but not very hard, and get the leglin down from the wall and stride over the sharn to the big cow Molly. "Get over, lass," and Molly would get over, and down Mother would sit and start to milk, slow at first, then faster and faster, the milk hissing, creaming, into the pails, the five cats sitting in a half-circle below, watching, or washing their faces, decent, and now and then giving a little mew, and the kittens dabbing at the big one's tails.

Father would bring in bundles of straw and throw them in the stalls in front of the kine, "A fine caller morning with wind in the loft. We'll need to take advantage o't. Can you hurry up the breakfast, lass?"

56

Mother would turn her head from the cow, "Hurry? And what do you think I'm doing now? Having a bit of a sleep in the greip?"

" 'Od no, you're fine. But just have the breakfast right on time. We're beginning the meikle Stane Field to-day."

So mother would be tearing down to the house in less than ten minutes, skirts flying, pails flying, nearly flying herself, crying to the boys "Aren't you up yet? Think shame of yourselves lying there and stinking. Out you get, Alick and Peter." Peter would grumble "Well, you told us to lie and not mess about in your road in the morning" and Mother would snap as she shot to the fire and stirred in handfuls of meal in the pot: "None of your lip, you ill-gotten wretch," and Alick would mutter "And none of yours," but awful low, Mother was a terror to skelp.

So out the two of them would get from the bed, gey slow, Oh God, it was awful, just a minute longer and they wouldn't have felt as though their faces would yawn from their heads. They'd have mixed up their clothes the night before as they went to bed, Alick would have lost his breeks or his scarf, Peter had kicked his boots under the bed, and they'd have a bit of a fight while they dressed, and Peter would say from his solemn fat face "Punch me again and I'll tell mother."

"Oh, aye, you would, you mammy's pet. You're worse than Keith."

"I'm not."

"You are. Who's feared at the kine? Who's feared at a punch? Even Keith could make you greet if he tried."

Mother would cry "None of your fighting. Alick, get out and open the hen-rees, and mind that you don't chase the chickens. Peter, come and give the porridge a steer. Are you wakened, my dawtie little man?"

You would whisper from the bed "Ay mother, whiles" it was true enough, sometimes you'd hear and see for a minute, then there came a long blank, you were swimming about, down into darkness, up into light of the cruse-lamp above the fire. But now Mother had dowsed that, it was

57

nearly daylight, through the kitchen window you could see far off the parks all grey in that early glim, waiting and watching like tethered beasts, with a flick of their tails the line of seagulls rising and cawing in by Kinneff. And Mother would pull out the meikle table, well-scrubbed and shining, and get down the caps, big wooden bowls with horn spoons, and lift the porridge pot off the fire, black and bubbling, pour out the porridge, set the great jug of milk in the middle and breakfast was ready and out on the close was the sound of the feet of father and Geordie coming for it, and behind them Alick, he'd let out the hens, nobody looking and shooed them and tried a new swear-word on them, and slipped into the stable, given Bess a pat, taken a draw at Geordie's pipe left alight in the top of a girnel, been nearly sick, walloped a calf that looked at him nasty-like in the byre, and eaten a handful of locust beans he'd nicked from the sack in the turnip-shed. And now he came looking as good as gold and quiet, and Mother said "That's my man. You're fair a help. Sit into the breakfast."

Then father would bow his head above the table, big brown beard spread out on his chest in tufty ends, and say the grace, decent and quiet:

> Our Father which art in heaven
> Hallowed be thy name
> And bless these mercies for our use
> For Christ's sake, Amen.

But the boys didn't know that these were the words and for years after that you would sit and wonder what God was doing with a chart in heaven and why father should swear at the end of the grace, folk only used the name of Christ when a horse kicked them head first into a midden or they dropped a weight on their toes and danced, or a flail wheeled round and walloped them one as they flung up an arm at thrashing-time. Only you knew Father couldn't be swearing, not really, else Mother would have been in a rage, instead of sitting there perky and quick, flaming hair,

58

Geordie Allison said if ever fire failed them here in the Maiden they could warm their nieves at the mistress's hair.

"So you're tackling Stane Park this morning then?"

Father said "Ay we'll be at it all day. Can you send out the dinner at twelve, would you say?" and Mother said couldn't he come home for it, like a decent man, he'd be tired enough, her eyes upon him in that way that she sometimes had, it made you ashamed that anybody should look at father, like that. But father shook his head, no time, they were far behind with the season as it was, must hash on ahead and try and catch up. "Ready, Geo?" and Geordie would nod "Faith, nearly, when I've sucked down the last of the brose. Right, Maiden, then, I'll be following you," he called father Maiden and it sounded queer till you learned that all the farmer folk were called by the names of the farms they had, you were glad that you bade in Maiden Castle and not at a place like Bogmuck, you thought awful to have folk call father muck.

So off the two of them would stamp together, up across the close to the stable door, the four horses standing harnessed within, champing and clinking, father would chirk "Come away, then, Bess" and Bess, at the furthest end of the stable would back down slow in her stall and turn and come showding down to the stable door. Behind her Sam and Dod and Lad, and as Bess came opposite Father would twist his hand in her mane and shove his boot in her swinging britches, and vault on her back with only a swing, Geordie couldn't, he'd to stop his horse and climb on with a stone to help, he said father was the swackest man he knew and folk wouldn't have guessed it, him stocky as that.

Through the close they'd ring and out into the road that led winding up to the heights of Stane Park, broom-surrounded, a woesome place, whins and broom and a schlorich of weeds had crept from the coarse land year on year as Maiden lay fallow as any maid; and this park Father set to break in with a double plough and fresh-sharpened socks, every day it was Alick's job to take socks and coulters to the smithy at Moss Bank for Sandy, the daft-like creature, to sharpen. So wild was the park with knife-grass and weeds, and great boulders that tried to lie down in the grass and scape the drive of the plough as it came. But midway the park were the stones from old time that gave the place its unco name, a circle of things flat and big, where the heathen had worshipped and had a fair time dancing, and singing and worshipping the sun, the foul creatures, instead of going decent to kirk with fine long faces and wearing lum hats.

And all about, the morning rising, other teams would be out in the parks, near at hand the straining teams of Balhaggarty shoring the slopes, team on team, with the gulls behind, their cries coming down the wind and the sound as the childe wheeled round the harrows and turned: "Gee up, there, wissh." "Come on, you brute." Beyond these slopes was a wink of the land of Badymick, Arch out in his fields, whistling, his whistle clear in the air, in the sky, him and the larks both daft together, whistling away for dear life up there, and a little dot trotting at the heels of him as he drove the sholt and the cow in the harrows, that would be Rachel, the daughter creature, small and sallow and a queer-like bairn to come of the red-faced stock of the Howe. Cruickshank's men one would hardly see except as Father turned at the foot of the park to go back up the drill and then he could see on the edge of the cliffs, poised between earth and sky in that light, the team that Cruickshank drove to work, a mule and a sholt and in front of them, tracing, the old wife herself, by God.

Father would take off his jacket and fold it and yoke the horses to the swingle trees and spit on his hands, high and clear the sky, the horses straining, waiting the words, "Come away then lass, come away then, Lad," off they'd go curling the furrow behind, and behind that Geo Allison sweating and swinging, one foot in the drill and another out, and crying to the Bees of horses to steady, God damn't, did they think they were hares, not horses? And the sun would be rising, the sea-mists going, wheeling, they would look down on Maiden Castle with its old walls skellaching over the sea and Father would think a minute, maybe: "That thing'll be dangerous, I shouldn't but say," but not severe or meikle disturbed, his was the nature to trust even a tower.

No sooner were the men folk out of the way then Mother was in a stew to get things redded up, hens meated, calves out, the kye new-bedded, the milk churned, Alick and Peter got ready for school, all at one and all at the same whip. And she'd do it too, like whirlwind, just, and Alick and Peter would be held and scrubbed till the skin gey nearly peeled from their noses and their breeks pulled up and their galluses fastened and asked if they'd been to the you-know-where, and they'd say, ashamed "Och, aye," even it if wasn't true; and Mother would say "Have you got your books? Here are your pieces and off you go. See you behave yourself with the Dominie."

They'd cry back "Och aye. Ta-ta, mother. Ta-ta, Keith" and you would run to the head of the courtyard where bare and white stone circles lay to take the stacks at the harvest's end: "Ta-ta!" and they'd wave and Alick, if Mother wasn't looking, would put his fingers to the end of his nose and spread them out and add the fingers of the other hand and stand on one leg and wheel round about, making fun of the Howe and Maiden Castle, the teams in the parks and the sun in the sky, he was fairly a nickum was Alick, said Geo Allison.

Father once caught him doing that and said " 'Od, laddie, is your nose so ticklish?" Alick said that it wasn't, but father said it must be and caught Alick under his oxter, gentle, and upended him and rubbed his nose in the earth, to and fro and Alick howled and father dropped him and stroked his beard: "I'll ay be pleased to help you, Alick."

Alick stood up and went away grumbling, but he said he didn't mind the old man, if it had been Mother caught him at that she'd have deaved the backside from a sow about it, him-disgracing-the-house-and-taking-the-Lord's-name-in-vain, just-awful-and-what-would-the-neighbours-say-about-it.

When they'd gone it was your chance to ransack the place and play the devil, and climb down the rock with hands holding the grass, down and down to the water's edge, the tide going out, far on the rocks shells and fine things littering the beach, fill all your pouches, there was a seagull, "Shoo away, creature" slow flap-flap it rose, yourself up the rock and round the mill-course and spread out your shells in the sun. By then the cats would have crept from the byre and come round in a circle to watch you a while, but whenever you'd your house with the shells built up they'd mew through the middle and knock it down, they were awfully ignorant creatures, cats.

You'd weary a while of the playing then, and lie flat on your back and look up at the sky, pale-grey, and wan in the slight spring sun, rooks cawing about the firs, high and far, caw-caw, unending; and there, a blink on the edge of the day, a thing like curtains sweeping on Maiden. You'd seen it before and knew what it meant and would race for the shelter of the cart-shed and watch, the curtain would wheel and the sun shine through, there rainbows glimmer and then the wash of the rain was pelting the roofs and sweeping up inland across the Howe, drooking the parks a minute, passing. Father and Allison wrapped a minute in the flay and sweep of the water, shining out next minute not hurted at all. It must be fine fun to be a man.

At eleven o'clock Mother would have made the dinner, porridge again, or stew of a rabbit, and loaded that into a pail and that into a great big basket with plates, four spoons, a bit of the kebbuck of cheese, a flask of the ale that she made herself; and slung the basket over her arm and cried "Come on, Keithie, we'll away with the dinner."

You hated her to call you Keithie, but trotting beside her her hand was kind, helping you up the chave of the road and on to the track that led to Stane Park. Father would see the two of you coming and draw in the horses at the tail of a drill, and Geordie Allison follow him in that, they'd loosen the harness and wipe down the horses and then come and sit under the lithe of the broom while mother dished the dinner out, sharp and quick with her scornful eye and her big red face and her thick-lipped mouth. "Ay, well, it doesn't look as though the two of you've done much in spite of all your haste to be out."

"'Od, woman, I'm sure we haven't been idle. What think you, Geordie?"

"Well, damn't, man Maiden, you must speak for yourself. Maybe you lay down and had a bit snooze, I didn't or else my memory's going."

"That'll do, Geordie Allison. Here, here's your plate. Fill up your gyte and give's less of your din."

And they'd all sit and eat, the horses nibbling grass, the sun flaring, the team in the other parks would have loosed and going swinging up to their biggings far off in the bothy of Bahaggarty some childe would be singing as he made his brose:

And Jean, the daft bitch, she would kilt
    up her coat
From her toes to her knees, from her
    knees to her throat
And say to her lad, as blithe as you
    please ———

And Mother would say it was just disgusting, those tinks of ploughmen and the things they sang, bairns hearing them too. You wished that you could have heard what the lass said, but father just nodded and said 'Od, aye, he'd never seen much fun in singing that kind of stuff about your lass, even though she's been as kind and obliging as the singer said, there was a time and place for these kind of pleasures, and the time to sing about them was when you were having them.

Mother would turn redder than ever at that and said "For shame, Maiden, you brute," and father give his beard a slow stroke and say "Well, lass, I've sang with you, and you with even less on your back than the lass in the song of that bothy billy."

Father was sore behind with his fields, but he was

winning as the Spring drew on, the Stane Field at last had been ploughed and harrowed, and a day came when bags of the new manure were carted from Stonehaven down to Maiden and from there out along the top of Stane Park and edgeways on to the long moor fields, two of them and the narrow one that fronted the sea and was needed for turnips. Father planned to manure the lot, the land had lain fallow in fine condition, but a touch of manure would kittle it up. And you would come out and watch them at it, still Spring, and still the fine weather holding, father swinging the hamper in front and broadcasting the manure with swinging hands, Geordie Allison toiling behind him and the sacks with a pail in each hand to replenish the hamper, the manure flying out in white clouds as they worked, shrill and queer down by the sea the clamour of the tide returning again, to you it seemed sometimes those afternoons would never end, on and on, till the sun at last, wearied with manure, sunk half-way down and looking out on the winding track that led to the Howe you would see two specks that moved and loitered and halted once a little way and stopped and considered, a long half-hour, Peter, Alick — coming home from school and digging out their boots from the ditch where they'd hidden them as they set out for school, Mother had intended them to be decent but at school the scholars had laughed at them, they went barefoot day in and day out and Mother would sometimes see their feet, at night and say "Well, God be here, however did you get your soles scratched like that?" And Alick would say "Och, we just had a game. Mother, can I have some supper now." And Mother would say "Supper at your age? Away to your bed, let's have no more of you."

But before that came had come loosening time, the four horses, unyoked from the harrow or ploughs and brought champing in through the cobbled close, caked with sweat, father in the lead as they stopped and drank at the meikle stone trough. "Steady on, Bess. Don't drink so fast," he was as careful of a horse at the tail of the day as he was of one at the early morning. But Geordie Allison would be crabbed and tired: "Come on, you old brute" he would say to Lad, "God Almighty what are you standing there doing. Praying?" and gave him a clap in the haunch that would send old Lad through the close at a trot and breenging like a one-year old into the stable. Father never said a word, for he knew Geo tired, as some folk could be, he himself never. So the two would meat the beasts in the half twilight and rub them down and water them, and straighten up and look at each other, and take down their jackets from the stable door.

"Ay, man, well, I think we'll away in for supper."

"Faith, Maiden, I think we've half earned it."

Summer and the cutting of the short wild hay, there'd be no time to lay down clover, Father got out a couple of heuchs and he and George Allison were at it all day on the long salt bents that rose from the sea beyond the peaked curl of the castled Headland. Then came broiling weather and the water failed inside the yard of Maiden Castle, the well went lower and lower each day till at last father had the roof taken off and he and Mother and Geordie looked down, the thing was old and green-coated, far down the water shone in half-mirk. Father took off his coat and went down, Mother watching, white faced, crying to him not be a silly-like gawpus now, as he usually was, and not spoil the water.

She and George Allison lowered pails while Father stood to the knees in mud and loaded the pails and had them pulled up, pail after pail through a long summer day, when he came up at last he was caked with dirt but canny and kind and calm as ever. "Aye, well, we'll tackle the rest the morn."

And tackle it they did, father again went down with a spade and pails and moiled in the half-dark and cleared out the mud and stones and dirt that clanjamfried the bent of the well. Geordie Allison pulled them up to the top and flung out each pailful over the dyke, spleitering out in the long wide arc to the boil and froth of the sea below, you thought it fun and at every throw let out a scream till Mother came running, flame-hair and red face gone white, and thrashed you because you had feared her so. And Geordie said when she'd gone to the house never to fear, you'd grow up yet and be able to thrash a woman himself, that would be some consolation like for the aching doup that you had at the moment.

So they cleared out the well and the water started slow to come in, Geordie Allison was made to load barrels in a cart and go up to the village and borrow there while father stayed and watched the well. And at first the water was a dribble, slow and then it came in jets and bursts, and father went down the rope to taste it and came back with his face a bit sober like. And he cried out "Lass," and mother came. "The water in the well — just have a look in."

So mother looked in and you did as well and nearly fell head first over the coping, seeing the pour and spray of it. And Father told Mother the water was salt, the sea had got in and the well was finished.

They sent off that night for a ploughman childe that sometimes worked on Balhaggarty, an old, slow stepping, quiet-like man, and he came down that evening as the light grew dim and chapped at the door and spoke to Father. And he said "Well, well, it's my wee bit stick you need, I doubt," and drew out a moleskin case from his pouch, the three boys crowding round to look. And inside the case was a bit of wood, no more, Alick said aloud what was the daft old gype thinking he was doing with that.

But he and Father went out from Maiden and walked slow up and down in the park out from the Castle where the headland rose. And after a while the ploughman childe pointed at the stick he held in his hand, it was wriggling about like a snake alive. "You'll find water here, and not over-deep. And my fee'll be five shillings, man."

Father said there was nothing else for it; and they dug the well through the month that followed, whenever they managed to get back from the work, digging and hafting in the evening light, Geordie Allison swearing under his breath by God when he fee'd he'd fee'd as a ploughman not as some kind of bloody earth-mole. But Father was the queerest man to work with, he never answered, just looked at him kind, with far away look that was somehow fey, and made a body fell silent to wondered, and felt ashamed to have vexed the man — aye, God, a queer character, Stratoun of Maiden.

And when at last the well was finished and sweet water flowing in Father said that they'd have a day off, what would Geo Allison do with the money if he had a ten shillings given him? Geordie said that apart from fainting with surprise he'd take the lot into Aberdeen and have such a real good blinding drunk he wouldn't know a known man's face. Father brought out his wallet and counted ten shillings into Geo's hand, Geo standing with his lower jaw hung down like a barn door that was badly used. Then he habbered "Well, Maiden, well man, this is fine," and turned and went off to the bothy room. Mother had seen and heard it all and she was in an awful rage at Father: "You heard what the creature said he would do?" And father gave his beard a bit stroke and mother a bit of a clap on the bottom "'Od, aye, lass, I heard, as I'm not very deaf. And what for no? Let every man follow the gait of his guts."

Mother said she never heard such coarse talk and father should be ashamed of himself, how would his bairns grow up to behave if they heard him say the like of that? Father said they'd no doubt trauchle long; and he didn't expect that Geo, sonsy man, would be as daft as behave as he'd said.

But faith, that was just what Geo did, next morning he wasn't to be found in Maiden, and the long red farmer childe of Bogmuck was out in the seep of the autumn morning, taking his ease, he'd had an awful night with eating over meikle salt fish to his supper, when he saw a man going over the hills, bapping it away Stonehaven way. And that man was Geo Allison and no other, he walked the whole way to Aberdeen, canny-like, to save his silver, through the Dunnottar woods of Stonehaven that scent in green all the countryside, Stonehyve itself was asleep as he passed but for a stray cat or so on the prowl and a couple of lasses that lay in the gutter, mill-lasses caught and ill-used by the fishers the night before, with their petticoats torn and their breasts sticking out, a dirty disgusting sight, Geordie thought, why couldn't the foul slummocks have stayed at home? They were just beginning to waken up but he paid them no heed and went shooting through, up the long road by Cowie and Muchalls, through Newtonhill with never a rest, the sun had risen and the teams were out, blue rose the smoke from the morning pipes as the scythe-men bent in rows to the hay, here and there Geo Allison would meet with a tink or a gentry creature in a fine bit gig, and he paid heed to neither rich nor poor and near two o'clock in the afternoon looked down and there under his feet was the grey granite shine of Aberdeen, smoke-clouded, with the smoke of the sea beyond, a gey fine place though awful mean, and as full of pubs and cuddlesome whores as the head of a Highlander full of fleas.

And Geordie started on the first pub he came to and worked on canny into Aberdeen, outside the fifth pub was a cart and horse and Geo jumped in and drove off in the thing, careering over the calsays a while till he tired of that and the folk all shouting, so he halted the thing in a quiet-like street and went into another pub, near and convenient, and said to the man "A nip of your best." And when the man drew the nip and set it down Geo of a sudden took a scunner at his face and gave the barman one in the eye to waken him up and teach him better than carry a face like that in public. It took the barmen and three other folk to throw Geo out on his head on the calsays, it did Geo no ill, he staunched the blood and crept round the back of a shed for a sleep, he woke up just as the dark was coming and counted his change, he still had four shillings. So he started in through the lighted street, and had here a drink and there a cuddle, pubs and whores as thick as he'd thought, then it all faded to a grey kind of haze, he'd a fight

68

with a sailor, and he and a lass had gone and lain on a heap
of straw, a gey fine lass though she thought him drunk and
tried to rape his pouches for him, he'd given her a cure that
cured her of that, and syne the mist had come down again,
he'd argued with a policeman, and held a horse and stood
in front of a stall for a while, singing, till they told him he'd
better move on; and at last, in one of the last of the pubs, or
thereabouts, he'd suddenly thought how full up this Aberdeen was of Tories, the scum of the earth, the dirty Bees.
So he started telling the pub about it, and next time he
woke up the stars were fading, a windy dawn grey over
Aberdeen, he was lying in a puddle of urine in the street,
and he'd been so thrashed and kicked about he thought for
a while he could hardly walk. But faith, he could, and
turned him about, and picked out the north star, and
turned his back, and started on the road for home again.

And that was Geo Allison's day in Aberdeen, Father
laughed when he told him the tale, " 'Od man, you got little
for your silver, I think." Geo Allison said that Maiden was
mistaken, he'd got a change, and changes were lightsome
as the monkey said when he swallowed the soda.

By September the Maiden Parks on the uplands were
rustling in long green-edged gear that every evening lost
some of the green and turned a deeper and deeper yellow,
though Stane Hill loitered behind the rest and scratched at
its rump and slept at its work and wouldn't waken, a real
coarse Park. Father went the round of them and looked at
the earth in the evening light, the crumbly sods and the
crackling corn and the rustle far down through the forest of
stalks as some hare lolloped off, filled up, to its bed. Above
the sky a shining bowl of porcelain, flecked and tinged in
blue, Father stroking his beard and nodding eyes far off on
the shining slopes where Auchindreich climbed up purple
into the coming of the darkness's hand. "We'll start the
cutting the morn's morn."

They hired a band of tink creatures from Bervie, ragged
and lousy and not over honest, they'd nip in the hen-houses

and steal mother's eggs if she weren't looking, the clothes from the line, the meal from the barn, and the dirt from under your fingernails. And Alick going in in the quiet of an evening to steal a handful of locust beans came tearing out with his face all red "Father, the spinners have been stealing the beans," in a fury about it, but Father not. He took Alick's ear in his right hand, soft, " 'Od, have they so? And not left some for you?" — Mornings, right on the chap of six, the bouroch of tinks were in Maiden close, waiting for the master the Geo Allison and the man they had hired from the village, warm, a cool wind up from the sea drifting through the clouds of the warmth as the lot set off for the Tulloch Park, or Joiner's End or at last Stane Muir.

And Father would halt inside the gate, the lot behind him, and take off his jacket, roll up his sleeves, and whet his scythe, the ring of it echoing up through the half-light, all the ground grey and dry and waiting, scuttle of little birds deep in the corn, Geo Allison whetting his scythe behind him and the man from the village with a spit and growl using his whetstone and telling the tinks to stand well back if they had the fancy to keep their legs. Then Father would bend and swing out slow, and cut and the sheaf of corn would swish aside, quicker and quicker, till at last he got the pace for the bout, behind him the other two following, uneven at first till they got the rhythm, the gatherers following, gathering and binding, quick and sure, their thin white faces straining and white, gasping as they flung the sheaves aside. Behind, if they looked up a dizzied moment they'd see on all the parks of the Howe the glitter of far scythe-blades, shining, gleaming, ay, man a fine sight, a real good harvest and the weather holding.

You would come out with Mother whiles when she brought the pieces for the harvesters, oatcake and ale and a bite of cheese for the gatherers, they called her Mem to her face, what they called her behind her back she never guessed, you did, you heard one and your heart nearly stopped, frightened and angry and wanting to cry. But for Geo and Father there were white sheaves and scones, milk

70

and great yellow dollops of butter, Alick and Peter were on school holiday and would come tearing in about as well and sit and stare and look fearfully starved, Mother didn't heed, if they couldn't stay and help in the parks they could wait for their dinners at the ordinary times.

Then one noon a great black cloud like the hand of a man fast-clenched in rage rose up above the shining humps of the Grampians far way in the east, across the haste of the harvesting Howe, folk stopped and stared at the thing and swore, it wheeled and opened and gleamed in the sun, bonny you thought it, only a kid, you didn't know better, Geo Allison swore "God damn't, that's the end of harvest to-day." The hand was unfolding and whirling west, a little wind went moaning in front like a legion of kelpies, the devil behind, over the hill of Auchindreich, the sun went, bright and shining a minute, dark the next, then the swish of the rain. Father cried to you "Run for the house, my man," you ran, legs twinkling in and out, fun to see your own legs twinkling, fell twice, didn't cry, too brave, you'd show the damned rain, couldn't catch you, there was the barn door and Peter and Alick standing inside crying "Come on, Doolie," they called you Doolie, and you them Bulgars under your breath, an awful word you mustn't let mother hear.

It rained for nearly two days and nights, the sea well frothed over and out of the streaming windows of the tower the sea looked like the froth of a soup tureen, far away as the evening closed the fisher boats of Stonehyve and Gourdon reeled into safety with drooked sails, the fog horn moaned down by Kinneff and the gatherers all went back to Bervie. Father sat in the barn, twisting ropes out of straw, Geo Allison or Alick fed the straw, father twisting, fun to watch, when you grew up you'd do that as well and be a big farmer and have a brown beard and marry mother and sleep with her and give her a smack in the bottom, like that, when she was in a rage about something or other.

You thought that the harvest was finished then, you'd stay in the barn day on day and twist up ropes, lonely playing, and listen for rats, Towser and you, he wagged his tail and cocked his ears and looked at you, sly, you the same, squeak the rat, the dirl of the rain swooping over the byres, go on for ever and when next Spring came you'd be a big man and go to school. But then the rain cleared off in a blink, late in the evening, father went out the round of the parks, you hung on his hand, still all the fields except that up in Balhaggarty a bothy childe was singing clear, to the soft drip-drip of the bending corn-heads.

The whins were a dark green lour in the light and father stopped and looked up at them, and smelt the wind, and looked down the fields at the glisten of the sea as it drew into dark and pulled its blankets over its head. And just as the two of you stood and listened there came a thing like a quiet sigh, like a meikle calf that sighed in sleep, grew louder, the wet head of the corn moved round and shook, father nodded. "Ay, fine, it'll be dry ere the morning, Keith."

And next day they started in on the harvest again, and got through it afore October was out, all cut and bound and set in stooks, great moons came that hung low on the plain above the devils stones in the old Stane Park while Geo Allison and father led by moonlight driving out Bess with an empty cart through the scutter and flirt of the thieving rabbits, the brutes came down in droves from the hills and ate up stooks and riddled the turnips, through the plaint and wheesh of the peesies flying, dim and unending through the moon-hush, to the waiting lines of the sound-won sheaves. Then they'd pack the carts full and plod back to the close and set to the bigging of the grain-stacks there, the harvest moon lasted nearly a week and one Sunday night Father looked at the sky and said they'd better take advantage of the grieve weather that lasted. Mother was in all her Sabbath clothes, she said to Father "Think shame of yourself. Lead on the Sabbath, there would come a judgment on us." Father said "Well, lass, maybe there will. But it's work of necessity and mercy, you ken," and mother said it was no such thing she was sure, but just clean greed, and whatever would the neighbours say?

But 'od, the creatures had no time to say a thing, the scandal of that night was soon all over the Howe, no sooner did dusk come down that Sabbath over all the touns than canny folk who had been to the kirk and stood up there right decent by the sides of their women, snuffling the Hundredth Psalm right godly, took a taik indoors and off with their lum hats and their good black breeks and their long coats with the fine swallow tails and howked on their corduroys and their mufflers and went quiet from their houses out to the stables, and yoked up the horses, whistling under-breath, and took out on the road to the waiting stooks. And all that night the Howe was leading, ere morning came there wasn't a standing stook in the Howe, all the harvest in and well-happed and bigged; and a man had time to sit down with his paper and read of the Irish Catholics, the dirt, them that wanted Home Rule and the like silly fairlies, the foul ungodly brutes that they were.

The Potato harvest was next on the go, Geo Allison said to Father, "Maiden, if we want to be clear of the rot this year we'll need to howk up and store fell early, I can feel in my bones a wet winter's coming." Father said Faith then, he was sorry about the bones, but it was real kind of them to give the warning, he and Geo would tackle the potatoes the morn. And so they did, Alick and Peter and Mother to help, you yourself ran up and down the drills and looked at the worms, big ones, pushing their heads out of holes and watching the gatherers, you liked worms, but Mother said "Feuch, you dirty wee brute" when you showed her your pockets full up of them. So you took them away to the end of the park and laid them all out on a big flat stone, they wriggled and ran races, fun to tickle them, but they wouldn't speak to you, they were awful sulky beasts, worms, when they were offended, like.

Geo Allison said that of all the foul coarse back-breaking jobs ever invented since Time was clecked potato-gathering was surely the worst, he'd a hole in his back above his dowp where his spine and his bottom had once joined on.

Mother turned right red when she heard him say that and told him "None of your vulgar claik", but father just said Geo must bear with the thing and fill up on fried tatties throughout the winter, funny man, father, Alick said he was daft, messing about with the drills at the end and going all over the land again and making as sure as a sparrow with dirt that there wasn't even a little wee tattie left, when Alick was big he wasn't to stay at home here, he was going to grow up and get a fee as a farm-servant on a place down the Howe, and drive big Clydesdales and every night go and sleep with a lass at the back of a stack, same as the Reverend Adam Smith did with his housekeeper.

That was at the end of the potato harvest he said that, the three of you sitting round the tattie pits, sorting out rotten tatties from the fresh, clean ones, a snell wind blew. And Alick boasted some more about what he would do, Peter listening half asleep as usual, you yourself began to speak as well, you said you wouldn't sleep with any body, ever, when you were big, but alone by yourself, and you'd be a cattler and look after bulls. And Alick said "Go away and not blether, Doolie," Alick was a cruel beast and you thought sometime when you were grown up, maybe ten or eleven, you'd get him alone you with father's gun, and blow off his head, right, with a bang, and that would teach him, that would.

But you caught a cold out by the pits that afternoon on November's edge, it closed and choked about your wind-pipe, Mother cried that God, the bairn was smoring when you sat at supper and caught you up, something red with a long forked tail seemed running and scuttling up and down your throat and then you saw father rise from the table, face all solemn, and cry to Geo Allison. Then you were taken off to bed, Mother's room, mother carrying you, sometimes you didn't like her at all, now — only with her safe and alone, if only she would hold you all the time, in darkness you woke and screamed for her and she held you close, funny texture her breast, smell of it, long hair about you, but the devil was back, fork-tailed, racing up and down your throat, low in the hush of one night you woke with the blatter of sleet on the window-panes, sudden in that hush the cry of an owl.

So you saw little or nothing of that year's end, Hogmanay for you was blankets, hot drinks, father's grave face, did he think you'd die? You closed your eyes a little and waited and then the funniest thing started to happen, the room and chairs began to expand and explode all about you, growing bigger and bigger, you looked at your arm, like the leg of a horse, you could see it swell and swell as you looked till it filled the whole room and blotted out everything, then Mother reached down shook you, "Keithie, here's your broth."

So Hogmanay went by, you heard skirling in the kitchen, somebody singing, somebody laughing, whistle of strange sleet one morning as you woke and looked out and there it was snowing white, ding dong out and across the happed lands, through the wavering pelt you could see from the window the smoke rise far from Balhaggarty, from the bouroch of trees that hid the kirk, black things, the crows, flying above it, oh, winter had come and you couldn't go out, you'd wanted to play in the snow.

Father said to the Doctor will the little'un die? and the Doctor was big and broad and buirdly, he'd ridden from Bervie on his big fat sholty, he shook his head "Faith no, not him. He's spunk in him, this bit son of yours, But he'll gang a queer gait by the look of him." Father asked how and the Doctor said "Faith, have you never used your eyes on him? He's as full up of fancies and whigmaleeries as an egg of meat, he's been telling me his dream and his fancies, — faith, that's a loon that'll do queer things in the world." Father said "Well, well, if he' does no ill, he may do what he fancies, I'll not bar his way."

But after that Father and Mother were queerer, they'd look at you queer now and then and syne nod, and you hear the story about the doctor and couldn't make out what they meant at all you'd just had a dream, every body had dreams. But you were growing up, oh, that was fine, a bairn no longer, to school next year, this first year at Maiden Castle put by.

BOOK II

SCHOOLING

As the New Year came blustering into the Howe, folk took the news of the parish through hand, standing up douce and snug in the bar and watching the whirl and break of the flakes that the wind drove down from the hills to the sea like an old wife shake the chaff from a bed. Ay, God there hadn't been a winter like this, said Gunn of Lamahip, since 'yt, he minded it well, he was fee'd at that time up in a place in Aberdeen, called Monymusk, one morning he woke and looked out of the bothy window, b'god, the farm place had vanished entire, nothing about but the shroud of the snow. So he'd louped from his bed and gotten a spade and hacked his way from the bothy door and set to excavating the lady, gey rich and stuck up, that owned the place. Well, he chaved from morning nearly till noon and at last got a tunnel driven through, and reached the front door and broke down that. And the lady said she'd seen many a feat, but never that kind of feat before, and raised his wages right on the spot and hardly left him a-be after that, maybe running in to see him in the bothy, he got scunnered of her after a while, though a gey soft keek and canty to handle —

Arch Camlin of Badymicks had come in, he said "God, Gunn, are you at it again? Cuddling the jades'll yet be your ruin." Gunn gave his great big beard a bit stroke, "Faith, man, it might once, but I've gotten by that. Did I ever tell you of that sawmill place that was owned by a countess creature in Angus. Well, one day she said to me, 'John, man'"

77

Young Munro, the nasty wee crippled thing said "Faith, she was making a doubtful statement," and Gunn turned round and said "Faith, and what's that?" and Munro said "That you were a man. Ay, God, Lamahip, you can fairly blow."

That was a nasty one for Lamahip, folk sipped their drams slow and squinted at them, and wondered if Gunn would take the crippled creature a bit of a bash on his sneering face to teach him better manners, like. But he couldn't well do that with a cripple, and God, it was doubtful if he'd understood the nasty bit insult of the nasty creature, he went stitering on with the tale of his women, folk yawning and moving away from him and watching from the window a childe or so coming swinging up from the storm-pelted road into the shelter and lights of the bar. There was Dalsack of Bogmuck that fine-like childe, his boots well clorted up with sharn, he'd been spending the day mucking out the cattle-court and came in now eident and friend-like and shy, and said to Craigan back of the bar "A wee half, Jim. Faith, man, but it's cold. Have you heard the newsy-like tale from Moss Banks?"

Folk cried out "No, what's happened down there?" and Dalsack took a bit sip at his dram and told them the tale, folk crowding about, God damn't, now wasn't that fairly a yarn? The poverty laird of Maiden Castle had got a right nasty clout in the jaw.

His horses had near gone off their legs with standing about the winter in the stable, snuffling at the scuffle of rats in the eaves and tearing into great troughs of corn, gey sonsy beasts, and he fed them well, him and that tink-like man of his, Geo Allison, ay, that was his name. Well, yesterday, when the snow cleared up, the Stratoun man had made up his mind to let out the horse for a bit of a dander, frost on the ground and a high, clear wind, and Geo Allison had set about the bit job, with the midden loons clustering at the stable door. The big mare had been led out by Allison, and the man was standing chirking at the door to cry out the others, all patient and fine when one of the loons, that big one Alick, had stuck a bit thistle alow the mare's tail. No sooner she felt that than, filled up with corn, her heels rose off the ground in a flash and planted themselves on Geo Allison's chest. He sat down saying un-Sabbath-like words, and b'god the world was full of horses' legs, the rest of the brutes, unloosed in the stable, no sooner heard the clatter of the mare's flight than they themselves tore like hell from the stable, scattering the two Stratoun loons like chaff, and careering round the court like mad, nearly running down Mistress Stratoun in the clamour. She cried to the brutes weren't they black ashamed, but damn the shame had one of the horses, they found the close gate and went galloping out, nearly tumbling head first down the old well, syne wheeling like a streek of gulls for the sea, gulls above it, cawing and pelting, Geo Allison scrambled up to his feet and tore after the beasts, crying to them to stop, the coarse Bulgars that they were and get their bit guts kicked in. Well, the mare was in the lead and she stopped and took a bit look out over the sea and syne another back to Geo Allison and kicked up her heels and took a bit laugh and turned and went racing across the ley field, making for the moor, the others behind her, and so vanished like the beasts with the chariot of fire, Geo Allison pelting like hell at their heels, folk living up here in the clorty north had only themselves to blame, the fools, instead of biding in the fine warm south.

Well, the horses fairly enjoyed themselves, they went over the moor of Balhaggarty and took a bit keek in at the kitchen window where Mistress Paton was making the sowans, she thought it was one of her churchyard ghaists and gave a yowl, and at that the mare gave back a bit nicker and showed her teeth and turned round, fair contemptuous-like and rubbed her backside against the window and ate a couple of flowers from a pot, and seemed to ponder the next bit move. Well, b'god, she'd soon a flash of inspiration, and raised up her head and looked over the hill to where the lums of Moss Bank were smoking, far away, a smudge by the tracks. And she gave another neigh and set off, the douce black plodding at her heels, gey quiet, the old gelding and the young mare skirting behind, stopping now and then to kick up their heels and look back at the figure of Geordie Allison, no more than a blue and blurring dot, far across the snow and turning the air blue as he cursed all the horses from here to Dundee, the daft-like dams that had given them birth and the idiot stallions that fathered them.

Well, you all know the kind of a creature Cruickshank is when he'll sight just one of your hens taking a bit of a stroll before breakfast and maybe casting one eye on his land. He was out at the tattie pits when he heard the coming of the Maiden horses like the charge of the cavalry at Balaclava, he looked up and cursed and turned white with rage. His wife heard the grind and clatter as well and came running out to stand beside him, the two of them just statues of fury, watching the mare nose round the close and nibble the hay from one of the stacks, and kick down a gate and look over at Cruickshank, one ear back and the other forward, a devil of a horse if ever there was one, just putting her fingers to her nose at him. But Cruickshank was fairly a skilly childe, he came out of his stance of sheer amaze and ran for the house and a pail of hot water and dosed it well with treacle and brought out slow across the close and put it in the middle of the cattle court. The smell was enough for all four of the horses, a bit thirsty and cold-like from their winter caper, they trotted nickering into the court and Cruickshank banged up the gates behind them and nodded, "Ay, well, when you next get out, it'll be with your owner's written apology."

Mistress Cruickshank cried "Ay, and his pay for the damage," and Cruickshank said "Get into the house. When I need your advice, I'll maybe ask for it" and they stood and glowered one at the other, frosty and big, fair matches for each other, till they both sighted Geo Allison coming dandering in about on the look-out for the Maiden horses. He cried out to ask if Cruickshank had seen them and Cruickshank glunched at him, Ay, oh, ay, he'd seen the coarse foul stinking beasts, where had the dirt come from, would it be?

Geo Allison was a bit ta'en aback ay that and said that they'd come from Maiden's, of course, where the hell else, out of the sea? At that Cruickshank told him he wanted none of his lip, but he could take home this message to his master: If he wanted his foul, mischeivous beasts he could come and get them, he'd not get them else.

Faith, Geo Allison didn't like the look of him and tailed away home with his tail 'tween his legs, and was hardly at Maiden than back came Maiden himself from his tear away over to Bervie. No sooner was he back than he heard the story, a funny devil Stratoun, and worth the watching. And all that he said was "Well, well, we'll see," and set out himself for the toun of Moss Banks.

The two of them met in the cattle court, Cruickshank had a straw skull full of neeps and was carrying them up to the door of the byre, big and squash, the sharn rising brown under his boots, when Maiden cried to him canny to stop. So he stopped and set down the skull, face black as thunder, and started in with hardly a pause for breath to ask what the hell he meant by it? Was this the way to treat an honest man, the stinking, half-gentry dirt that he was? Mistress Cruickshank came tearing out to watch, and all three looked at Stratoun and they thought him gey feared, he stood stocky and quiet, giving his beard a bit stroke, and syne nodded "Well, well, I'm sorry for that. But I doubt I'll need my horses back again."

Cruickshank said "You'll get them back when you pay for them," and Maiden just stood and shook his head, "Faith, no man, I'll take them back just now," and sure as death there'd have been murder then, Cruickshank was just taking off his coat and Maiden was fairly a sturdy billy, but that Alick, the biggest of the Maiden sons, came tearing through the yard at that minute, crying "Father, father, you'v got to come home. Keithie's ill again, and spewing up blood," his mother had sent him, he'd run all the way. Stratoun turned round and went striding out of the close and across the hills, the loon at his heels, forgetting everything about the horses.

Geo Allison would have tailed out after him but that Cruickshank cried "Hey, what's your hurry? You can surely lead a pair of them back yourself. I'll take the other pair back for you." And while Geordie Allison stood and gaped b'god Jim Cruickshank lead out the horses that he'd sworn he wouldn't part with at all, and got ropes to lead and followed Geo, and they sludged back douce across to the Castle, and stabled the horses up slow and quiet, not to raise a din with a the bairn sick. And when he had finished with doing that Cruickshank went down to the kitchen door and lifted the sneck and went cannily in and asked Mistress Stratoun was there anything he could do, they hadn't a sholt here at Maiden, should he drive down to Bervie and bring up the doctor?

And what thought you of that of the Cruickshank childe? For off to Bervie b'god he had driven, as anxious to help with the saving of the loon as he'd been to knock John Stratoun's teeth down his throat a bare half hour afore. Faith then, when he'd broke down the ice there would maybe other folk go down to Maiden, an ill-like thing with the bairn dying, 'twas said he wouldn't last out the week.

III

Drift and coloured clouds and a long queer time that you tripped and stumbled, shamble and slip, down a long cave that was littered with bones, dead men here, dead men there, thick air so you couldn't breathe, choking and stumbling for lack of breath down and down to the dark of the cave. And then you were out, for a minute up, and opened your eyes, and there was mother, funny man beside, with a basin all blood, awful stuff blood, it must be the doctor, they did coarse things to little loons, you screamed and screamed while they held you and soothed you, and you fought some more and went back to the cave.

Alick and Peter, as they told you later, could hardly sleep for the din you raised, like a calf with the scour, and them both so sleepy. And they couldn't get to their beds that night, anyhow, for the gallons of hot water that had to be boiled on the open fire, Mother flying about the place with her skirts kilted up and her face all red, flinging the furniture out of her way, not safe to be anywhere near the daftie, Alick had whispered low to Peter. Father had just sat down in the chimney-corner, Geo Allison over at the other side, there was nothing they could do and they took it calm, but mother was all in a fash that when the doctor came down he could wash his hands and the blood from the knives he'd been cutting you with, and not find the place looking like a bit of a barn. Father gave her a pat on the bottom "Don't fash, it'll come to all the same in the end. We've all of us got to pass some time, and he's the only one that we've lost."

Mother rounded on him in an awful rage: "Who've we lost? He'll outlive you all, and do things in the world you'll never do." Father said "Well, well, if that's the case, why are you getting ready to rub down the corpse?" and Mother told him not to be a daft fool, this wasn't for a corpse, but the doctor man.

And when he came down he was washed and fed and said he thought you'd maybe survive, and Geordie Allison trying to be newsy, struck in "Och, ay. There's a lot of killing in a kyard," and mother gave him a look that nearly blasted him, you were always Mother's pet, yes you were.

Well, it was that night while you were sleeping and the snow was on again, that the village began the first of its visits, Dalsack and his Edith, the housekeeper lass, came down from Bogmuck, stitering through the drifts, Dalsack with a load of a kebbuck of cheese, for the invalid, like, and Edith with a pot of jam, Mother had heard all about her, a

Real Coarse Quean, and was maybe a bit short when they were shown in. But losh, Peter thought her awful bonny, he'd sleep with her when she'd grown up, she'd red hair and fine round legs and arms, and she sat down and hoisted up her skirts and warmed herself at the fire and spoke and Mother thawed out, and sat down for a rest. And no sooner had she done that than Edith herself jumped up to her feet and started getting a meal ready for them all, Mother that wouldn't let another help gave her a nod, "Oh ay, if you like". Dalsack and father were at it on the land, about the best time to muck it and the short-eared corn, would it be a decent crop in the Howe? And just as they were getting on fine there came another scuffle at the sneck and in came stamping the Cruickshanks of Moss Bank, Father and Mother and another one. Mother would hardly speak to them at first and she and Mrs Cruickshank eyed one the other like a couple of hens about to fight, Mrs Cruickshank big as Bess, gey near, and with an awful face to match; but Father cried her into a seat and they all sat down, and the third one from Moss Bank, a young-like childe, was introduced, awful exciting, you couldn't guess who he was . . . You said yes you could, and Alick said you couldn't, you were lying upstairs all cut up with knives and dripping blood like a new killed pig. So you couldn't guess, see? . . . And the man was the son of the Cruickshanks, William, that had been a jeweller up in Aberdeen and had run away and joined the soldiers and fought all over the world, Blacks, and Chinese, awful brave, when Alick was grown up he'd do the same, steal things from jewellers, only he wouldn't be such a fool as get caught. So *he* sat down as well, and the old Cruickshank cuddy and Mrs Cruickshank, hell, what a face, and they claiked and claiked till they wearied the lads, Mother wouldn't let them go to their beds in the corner, it wouldn't have been decent, though they were nearly yawning their heads off with sleep and pulling up the corners of the blind and squinting out at the ding of the snow, the squeege of the sea worse than ever that night, like the kind of daft beast you'd said it was like.

Father had cried out to Peter to ask " 'Od man, you're gey white about the gills. What is't that's got you?" and Peter, the fool, had told the story you'd whispered in bed, before you were ill, of the ill beasts without eyes, great slimy worms, who rose from out the sea in the night, wet squelch and scuffle over the Maiden walls, snuffling blind hungry, a grue in the dark. And all the folk in the kitchen listened, and looked a bit as though they'd grue themselves, Mistress Edith gave a shiver and covered her eyes and old Dalsack even took a keek over his shoulder at the rattle and smoulder of the black night wind snarling outside the kitchen door, for a minute they all listened, even father, to the whoom of the storm in the lum, beneath it, below it the surge of the water rising up from the caves of the sea, even Mother had her red face queer a bit, with its flitting eyes and that nasty smile frozen on her jaws, and the Cruickshank fright neighed out it wasn't canny, a laddie like that, not much wonder he was lying up ill. But Father just smiled placid at his pipe and so did Jim Cruickshank, they didn't fear anything, Alick thought it was a pity they hadn't had that fight he'd stopped when he brought the news of your illness, they'd plenty of guts for a fight the both of them.

Then William Cruickshank, that was sitting by Dalsack's housekeeper, Edith, started to tell of the queer fairlies he'd seen and heard in India, an awful antrin place, the creepers came down and moved at night with things like hands of flesh, if a man was caught in a jungle alone those coarse-like plants would strangle him. And he told of the heat and the thirst of the days, the pallor at night like spilt butter-milk, buttermilk sprayed on a summer midden, full of ill smells, about the trees watching and waiting, the thump of your heart nearly sickening your stomach, and far off down the bit track you had took the thump and thud of following feet, following quick and sharp on your track through the glow and flow of the moonlight, daren't look back, could only go on, maybe a tiger, maybe worse, he himself had once been tracked that way, he could hear the pad of the beast close behind and at last he swung round and faced and God —

And Soldier William stopped when he got to there, cheery and buirdly, but his voice now solemn, you'd have heard a pin drop, and Mistress Edith behind him was gripping his arm, he looked down at her hand and then at her face and gave the hand a pat, she mustn't fash, guess what the bloody thing was after all? Only a wild pig, a sow at that, maybe tame once and grunting at his heels in the hope he'd have a bit offal to give it? But Jesus, it nearly had turned his wame!

That was a fine enough story, eh? but his father that silly old sumph, Cruickshank, God who would have him for a father, said sharp "Ay, maybe you've had your adventures, that's no reason to take the Redeemer in vain. If you've come home to bide at Moss Bank with us you'll bide as a well-favoured, God-fearing lad." And even Peter and Alick felt shamed, Moss Bank speaking that way to a grown-up man like his son, but he didn't seem shamed, just laughed and said in his English-like way "Don't worry, father, I feared God enough that night when I thought the tiger was with me." And then he told another story that mother and Cruickshank both thought right fine, about a soldier in his regiment, a decent-like chap, who'd said he was an atheist, didn't believe in God. Well, he caught a fever and was taken to a hospital and his last words were "Give me the Book." And when he asked "What book" he said "There's only one Book — my bank-book, of course," and then laughed at them, the coarse devil had known they expected he'd say the Bible. And he'd died right like that, an awful warning.

Mother said "Yes, the foul stinking swine", Alick said she would like to cut folks throats for Jesus, so would Moss Bank, they both looked as solemn as hens choked on dirt, but Alick took a look at the soldier, William, and he was looking at Mistress Edith and just at that minute he gave her a wink, and Alick looked at the others then, Father was staring up at the couples, Geo Allison was blowing his nose gey loud, Alick said to Peter in bed later on he thought that that soldier Bulgar was just making fun of Mother and Moss Bank. And whether that was true or not he'd no right to look at Edith like that, Alick himself was to have her for his lass when he'd grown up and robbed some jeweller and pushed mother off the Maiden cliff, so he would sometime, he was sick of her nagging, and owned Maiden himself when Father was dead, so he would, Peter and you would be just his ploughmen, he was the eldest.

Well, they'd all had a late bit supper then and Mother gone up to have a look at you, and Mistress Edith with her, tall, and ruddy, you'd opened eyes to the dazzle of light, stopped your blowing of little red bubbles, to stare at the woman beside Mother, bigger, with her fine face and laugh, she whispered "Poor man, oh, poor wee man" and you stared and stared and tried to speak and then tumbled in to the cave again. But Mother had thought you were getting on fine, and taken Mistress Edith down again, a meikle supper spread in the kitchen, ham and oatcakes and some of the Dalsack cheese, and father sat in to say his grace and they all ate up and had a claik, Dalsack said with his shy, fine smile "That must be an extraordinary laddie, your youngest, Mistress Stratoun," and Mother said "Och, just ordinary, ordinary" she didn't want folk to think you queer. But Geo Allison said b'god you weren't that, with the queerest havers and stances and answers, a funny bairn, no doubt you'd get on, into a daftie-house, maybe in the end. Father said "No fear of that. Though, faith, I will say he's a queer-like nickum. He'd speir the head from a Devil Stane or a creel of fresh herring back into the sea. 'Od, he'll be a handful to the teachers, I warrant, when we send him up to the village school this Spring."

You'd always remember till the day you died that queer, quiet evening in middle March that father took you out to the fishing, the first evening you'd been letten out, pale for a breath of air, Father wrapped you up in a blanket and carried you, rod and tackle over one arm, you over the other, the sun had gone down saffron behind except for some tint on the verge of the sea, it was sleeping in a little foam of colour and far away on the dying edge of the white wings of the Gourdon fleet went home, you stared and stared at it all, at the quietness that was rising a dim wall in the east, creeping up the sky and overtaking and drowning in blood the lights behind the fisher boats. Father set you down and stepped in the boat, tucked you up, and sat down and picked up the oars. "Fine, Keith lad?"

You said "Ay, father," and looked over the thwarts to the little hiss of the water, out, down to the shag and sway and green gleam of the bottom of the sea where the fairlies bade. But there were none to be seen at this, it was clear and open and you looked up and saw far along the fringing cliffs the place where the seagulls wheeled and cried out over the brinks from Dunnottar Castle it came on you this was maybe the sea, the beasts only silly dreams after all, light and the gulls and white hiss of the sea. Your stomach still felt awful funny inside you, as though Bess the mare had stepped on it, the smell of the sea made it turn a wee, but you didn't let on, Father would have turned and taken you back.

Instead he took the boat out to the point, beyond it, suddenly, the evening wind came, it blew a little spume in your faces, your nose and cheeks stung to its touch, a little smother of blood on the sea, soaking and pitching under the keel, Way way way! the gulls crying. You said "Father, why do they aye cry that?" and he stopped and listened from unlimbering the tackle, "Cry what, my mannie" and you told him "That — Way, way, way!"

Father said well, 'od, he didn't right know, the beasts and birds had funny-like cries, it was maybe some kind of speaking of theirs. You said "Oh. But have they all lost their way?" and father gave you the funniest look, he said that you were a gey queer lad, and bent to his tackle and then straightened again, listening to the gulls and stroking his beard, the sunset behind him on the sea.

You drowsed a bit then and opened your eyes, father

was pulling a fish aboard, a great gaping brute that blinked at you and worked its jaws and floundered and gasped, you drew up your legs away from it, Father didn't notice, the beasts were coming in bourochs, fast as he let down the lines for them, blue and grey rising out of the sea, fluttering and flicking, paling and dying, now the great wall behind the horizon's edge had blackened and blackened as though some Geordie Allison out there with a pail and tarbrush in the other hand had mistaken the sky for the barn wall, through the tar there came a glimmer of a star funny things stars, lights far away, God lighted them at night with a spunk from the box in a pocket of his breeks, striding backwards and forwards the roof of heaven, he'd a long brown beard like Father's just, but he wasn't so fine, sometimes you were dead feared of him. Father turned round "Not cold are you then," and you said you weren't, neither you were, just frozen in a wonder looking at the sky, arching and rising in the coming night. What if God made a bit slip some time and cracked the sky and came tumbling through, box of spunks still gripped in his hand and splashing the water so high from the sea it went pelting high up across the Howe —

And then you were feared, you held your breath, tight, there was the crack, growing wider and wider, a splurge on the lift, the dark behind, light in front, the splurge blue and yellow, the gulls had stopped that daft crying and crying and the wind had stilled, why didn't father see, He was coming, He was coming.

Boom!

Something flickered from the crack, and father raised his head.

" 'Od, we'll need to be holding back. There's the thunder, Keith, it'll frighten your Mother."

That thunder-pelt was the beginning of the wettest Spring that had come on the Howe for many a day, all that night it thundered and rained, in turn, when one had finished with splitting the sky and scarting its claws along the earth and over and through the dripping parks, the other came down in blinding pelts, the swash of it warping through roofs and walls, the cattle court of Balhaggarty was flooded out and half the stock drowned, at Moss Bank Sandy the dafty had come home gey late from a boozing ploy and gone into the smiddy where the coals still glowed and sat him down for a bit of a warm before sneaking up the stairs to his bed. And faith if he didn't fall fast asleep and was woke with a smack of cold water in his face, the smiddy swirling with a thing like a wave, he thought between the coals and the water he was surely in hell at last, not fair and went yammering out of the place to the kitchen door of Moss Bank to beat and clamour till letten in by his brother William who'd been the soldier. William asked what the hell was he up to, the fool, screeching around like a sheep half-libbed, and Sandy yabbered and dribbled and shook and said that coming by Dalsack's, he minded, he'd heard an awful commotion and cry and decided the devil was in there at last, getting at Dalsack for sleeping with his housekeepers, but he'd never thought Auld Nick would follow him here.

William said "Here, what's that that you say. Dirty lout," and near bashed him one, Mistress Edith a fine and upstanding girl that wouldn't look at a rat like Dalsack. But Sandy only moaned and yabbered some more, and at last Will put on his breeks and leggings and his reefer coat and set out for Moss Bank, near blind with the flare of the lightning sizzling and pelted with a slow dry wind that blew steady and strong, 'twixt the gusts of rain. In the Bogmuck kitchen a light was shining, he chapped at the door and went in and found out then what the commotion was about, Dalsack had had water taken in his kitchen, with a fine pipe and the Lord knew all the arrangements, and been a bit proud at being civilised: but early that night as they went to their beds the whole damn arrangement had burst in the rain, that was the commotion that Sandy had heard, the bed of the bairns in the kitchen drenched, Dalsack had come tearing down in his sark, naught else, and tried to light a candle, and the bairns had thought that he was the devil, coarse tinks creatures to think that of the man because he had whiskers like a yard of broom, syne Edith had come and tried to comfort them, and stop the flow of the water from the pipe, from them, an awful soss. Well, William was a skilly man with his hands, he'd learned in the Army to do all kinds of things from mending a pipe to cutting a throat, he shot about and stopped the flow, and took a sly look at Edith in her nighty wet, it stuck to her bonny chest with the points of the nipples sweet and showing, wet hair down her back like a Viking maid, by God, he made up his mind at that moment he'd get her and have breasts, hair and all, though the whole of the Howe was to be one long howl. Dalsack smiled shy through his whiskers and sark and said he was awful obliged to him, a fine childe, Dalsack, he dug out the whisky they sat drinking that till the morning came and William would stride back again to Moss Bank, through a Howe that was just a soss and a puddle and under the lour of a sky like lead.

And going back he followed the ridging track and went round and through by the Auld Kirk lands, and there a gey antrin sight met his eyes as he looked over into the old kirkyard where the folk of the Village had been laid in earth since ever the memory of man began, there ere old stones there that leaned this way and that, with daft-like inscriptions and curlicues, stones from the days of Christ's Covenant, one with a picture graved in the stone of an old-time brig in full sail, fair daft, that had been the ship of a Captain Stratoun; and the grass grew high and rank and dreich, choked round with the flat, bland blades of docken, a fine kirkyard and seldom disturbed except for the hares that had their holes there, maybe lairing there young in some coffin place in the bones of a woman once young and bonny, as Geddes Munro, the cripple, had once said, the foul young beast, so William remembered, he'd said it no doubt for a spite of the fact he'd never lair *his* body in any woman's. But now as William Cruickshank looked over the wall under the drip of the dreich dark yews, it looked like a hotter in a cattle shed, stones had been flung down here and there and a tide of water swashed through the place, flinging up the end of a new-buried coffin, that would be the coffin of a joskin man from the Home Town back of the village. In the thin wet glimmer of the March morning it looked an evil and fervid place, and Will Cruickshank shivered and turned in a half-run till he saw something that near made him sick, the figure of a woman over by the church wall, pressed up against it, a woman in white, in a nighty, hair down about her shoulders, bonny-gleaming, and weeping and weeping as though her heart would break. God damn't, what was she doing there? For it was the Reverend James Dallas's wife.

Well, he nearly stept over to question her on't, and was just giving his soldier's mouser a twist afore he did that, a fine figure of a man, when she turned and went out of the place by herself, bare-footed, he saw the gleam of her bare feet, she passed down into the shelter of the avenue trees, the morning was hardly breaking, white, he stood with a prickle of skin and stared after, had he really seen her or was it a fancy?

So he went back to Moss Bank and told the tale of the riven kirkyard, but not of the weeping minister's wife, he kept that till later, and Moss Bank said it was the just the kind of a thing that would happen in a proud and sinful place like an Auld Kirk, you'd not find the like of that in the field where the Reverend Adam Smith buried the Free Kirk men. And just as he said that the postie came in about, young Munro with his white, sneering face, and asked if they'd heard the news from the Howe? They hadn't, and so he began to tell them, — they knew of that daughter of Gunn of Lamahip, Queen, the dressmaker, so dark and stuck-up, a Gypsy-like bitch with her quiet airs? Well, where do you think she had spent the night? — at her shop in the village, not going home, she said that coming on of the storm had stopped her. Faith, maybe so it had, but did that account for the fact that as the morning broke and the Dominie's servant lassie, Kate, was getting up with a

wearied yawn and taking a keek down the street she saw
the door of Queen's shop slide open and who should come
out, rubbing his eyes, unshaven, with a gey dreich look on
his face, but the Reverend Adam Smith himself, that fat
coarse ill-living Free Kirk loon. — Cruickshank of Moss
Bank said "G'way with your lies," but young Munro just
sneered at him coarse. "Lies? Fegs, there was lying enough
there last night — your Free Kirk man in the bed of Queen
Gunn."

And afore that Saturday was done the news of the ploy
was all over the parish, men meeting one another on the
top of boxcarts cried it out, they cried from hedges and
stacks, and the tops of barns they had set to repair, at
Balhaggarty Mrs Paton greeting in her dairy where all her
cheese had been spoiled by the water and the eggs piled up
like a ready made omelette, dried up to listen to her servant
lass, and then ran to carry the news to the elder, Sam
Paton, solemn, rubbing his stomach, he's awful pains
below his waistcoat this morning, he said it was just the
kind of thing he expected to have happened to a Free Kirk
minister, and rubbed his stomach some more and looked
round, and went down to Maiden to see how they were, so
he said, but really just to pass them the news, awful kind of
him, Mrs Stratoun said, ay, God, a right handsome bitch of
a woman and had brought three fine sons intil the world,
though they said that the youngest one was a daftie.

The storm had nearly missed Maiden Castle, except the
loft where Geo Allison bade, Geo said that it smote in on
him at midnight like the angel of God, by the look of his
face he and the angel weren't on good terms, he sat and
shivered the day by the fire. When he heard the story of the
two bit kirks, the auld one with its dead in resurrection and
the Free one with its minister acting spry and quick, he said
he expected that from ministers, did they ever work like
other folk and use up their juices and go tired to bed? —
Not them, they'd had to be randy to live. John Stratoun
said 'Od, that might be so, but he hardly saw that the fact
would account for the Reverend James Dallas at the least

93

getting out of his bed in the middlle of the night and tearing up a coffin or so, just to prove that he was a vital man. And Sam Paton gave his stomach a bit rub, and a glower at Geo Allison, sour as his wame, and said he'd no liking for blasphemy. And Geo Allison mumbled "Your stomach won't stand it," but not over loud, he was only a joskin and not a gey big farming man.

The only place in the Howe that day that hadn't heard the two scandals till late was Archie Camlin's at Bady-micks, the couples of the byres had tumbled in and nearly killed a couple of his kye, and Arch was up in the roof giving them a mend with wee dark Rachel standing below, carrying the nails and her eyes on Arch as though on Elijah coming from the clouds when Sandy Cruickshank took a wamble in there and cried up the news, teething and dribbling and mouthing. Arch said b'god he saw nothing in that, couldn't the Reverend Adam have a sleep where he liked or the dead in the kirk of the Reverend Kames go out a bit stroll if it took their fancy? "Get away home, Sandy, man, to your bed, and not blether that kind of dirt to me with the lassie there standing by and listening." Sandy looked at Rachel and mouthed and yammered "She over-young to understand" and Arch called down "Away home with you. Bairns ken well enough from the womb, I think, all the ways that got them there. And I've little fancy for her growing up to snigger and sniffle around every tale of every auld childe that sleeps with a woman." So off poor Sandy had to waddle through the glaur, all the thanks that he got for his story, and what did Arch Camlin mean by his say, would he have the quean Rachel grow up a fair heathen and not know the difference between right and wrong?

Next day there was such a power of folk in Free Kirk at ten as hadn't been there since the news of Balaclava, near, the Reverend Adam climbed into the pulpit and peered down at them over his stomach and the two-three chins he wore over his collar, and puffed, and then drew out his great hankie, and blew a blast on it like the Last Trump's blast, and then preached them a sermon from Numbers, fegs, all about figures and descents and ascents and a creature called Jeanie Ology, would she be one of his lasses, would you say? It was more than likely, but heard you ever the like, him introducing into the pulpit the name of another lass after that night he's spent in the cuddles of Queenie Gunn.

The Auld Kirk itself was nearly toom, the Reverend James Dallas preaching bitter on the traipse that creature Lot had had when he went out of the City of Sodom, there was hardly a soul in the pews that day, pine shadowed, the sun shone through flying blinks of rain, forward under the pulpit head the choir sitting upright, genteel, behind them the pew of the Badymicks folk, Arch Camlin there with his little lass, and God she had a right unco stare, her with her boots and her funny limps and her dark-like skin, like a nigger's near, you couldn't wonder if the mother in law wasn't so keen about the bit creature. Midway was the pew of the elder, Sam Paton, with his wife prinked out in all her braws and jingling when she moved like a horse at a show, and behind that the seat of the Lamahip folk, would you believe there was Queen Gunn sitting there distant and quiet and dark, her eyes staring out of her face like live lumps of coal, only quiet coal, up at James Dallas as he preached from the pulpit, down from him to the seats in the corner where sat the folk from the manse themselves, the mistress and her bit maiden Ella, and further back still in their gentry's pew, the folk from Maiden, John Stratoun himself and his red-faced wife her head bent genteel but her eyes sharp and flitting on everything about her, their three weans beside them, all dressed up and starched. And over and above them all there thundered the tale of that creature Lot, his life, his death, and the coarse thing she'd done with that daughter of his in a bit of a cave. Folk put up their hankies to hide their yawns and poked their bairns to keep them awake, all except Arch Camlin with his dark quean Rachel, her head had fallen forward on the desk in front, sleeping the creature and over the way the youngest of the Stratouns sleeping, as well, that laddie that had nearly died a month back.

Ah well, they were gey young for the kirk. They were going to school inside the next week, and fegs that would waken them up for good.

You thought it an awful funny place, the school, the Dominie was big and bald and thin, with glasses perched on a long thin nose, he stood in the playground between the two walls that separated the lasses' playground from the lads', and rang a bell and afore you could blink there were scholars tearing in from all directions, out of the hedges and over the walls, and tearing out of the lavatories where they'd been drawing funny pictures and up from the post-office tattie-pit where they had been throwing things at the post office, big loons and little ones and medium ones, and lassies with long plaits and legs, didn't like it, thought you'd maybe cry for a bit, and felt awful lost till you sighted Peter. You ran to him and took his hand but he was ashamed and pushed you away and said "Your place's with the bairns, see?"

So you'd to line up last of all the lines and were awful ashamed, they put a lassie beside you, little and dark, and she looked at you queer and you stared down at your boots, fine boots, Mother had brought them in Bervie for you. And minding mother you nearly cried again, till you thought of the piece that you carried in your bag, for dinner, bread and butter and jam and a big soda scone with treacle inside it. So maybe you'd like the school after all.

Inside Miss Clouston took the little ones, she was awful thin and stern and fierce and the scholars said she wore red drawers and kept her strap in brine to pickle, she wasn't young, and looked about a hundred, and if one of the little ones messed up the floor she'd flush up red and say "Dirty, go out" and near frighten a little 'un out of its life. But she didn't with you, she liked you from the first and was awful kind and took you to the fire and you warmed up and newsed with her and told her of the fish father catched in the sea, and had she ever seen the Maiden Mare Bess, losh, yon was a horse, last month you were ill, it was awful queer, the doctor cut you, you liked better sleeping on your own for all that, had the Missie ever slept by herself, did she ever hear the queer beasts at night that came creeping up out of the sea, snuffle and slide, Father said they weren't real, hadn't that loon a funny face, "My brother Peter says you wear red flannel drawers".

Miss Clouston said sharp "Well, that'll do, Keith. Now sit down here beside this wee girl, her name's Rachel, and see you don't fight." So down you'd to sit beside a lass, fight, you wouldn't fight with a quean, and you said right out that Alick said a quean couldn't fight a kipper off a plate, they were over weak in the guts. And there was a snicker of laughing all about and next minute you thought your head would fall off, Miss Clouston had smacked you so hard in the ear, she was a bitch and you cried a bit.

And while you were doing that and Miss Clouston, red faced, was taking the first of the lessons, singing, they'd all to stand up and she banged the piano and said "Do Ray" and they all said "Do Ray" the little quean Rachel tugged at your sleeve and said not to mind and not to be feared, she herself wasn't feared at any one. So you dried your nose on your sleeves and said you weren't feared, you weren't feared at anything, one night you were out, it was awful dark and a great big dog had come leaping to bite you, and you'd taken an axe and killed it dead, you were gey strong. Rachel said "Oh losh, that was awful brave" and you told her some more of the things you'd done till Miss Clouston barked "No talking there among the little ones," that meant you two and you just sat wearied.

But syne she started lessons for you two and drew three funny pictures on the blackboard and told you to draw them as well, awful hard, they looked all wrong, one was a funny man called A, standing the way father sometimes stood, and another B, would that be the daft Bee that Geordie Allison would call the horses, the third was C, and was just daft, sea wasn't like that, oh, it was awful school, you minded sudden the sea and its greensy splurge out over

97

the rocks and the gulls crying. But then you saw Rachel was drawing the daft-like stuff on her slate, so you had, and some more after that, and it wasn't so bad, though you fell asleep afore dinner-time.

At dinner you sat at the foot of the playground on the edge of the hedge and listened to Alick saying what he'd do to a lad, Jockie Elrick, that had said that he could fight Alick easy. And Alick finished his dinner quick and said to Peter "Look after Ma's Pet" he meant you, and took out a great gully knife from his pouch and started to sharpen it on the sole of his boot, loons standing around and gaping at him, he was going to libb Jockie Elrick with it and then cut his throat from ear to ear, so he said, you cried out "Ay, hurry up," for you'd never seen that done afore to anyone. And over at the other side of the playground Jockie Elrick was sharpening his knife as well, the lads all said there'd be an awful lot of blood.

But the bell rung afore they could get to grips, and you'd the long afternoon to get through. Miss Clouston brought you a book of pictures, one was a train, you'd like to drive a train, and one was a beast that you didn't know, like a great big dog. Rachel knew more than you, she spelled it out and said it was a lion, her father had told her a lot about lions, they bade in a place called Africa and ate up black men, you asked why, it would surely be nicer to eat white, Rachel didn't know, that was just the way with lions. And then Miss Clouston called "Children, you mustn't talk," so you had a little bit sleep instead, and woke up with Alick shaking you awake, he'd come to take you home your first night.

The bairns were pouring out of the school and down in the playground going mad with delight at being freed from the Dominie and Missies, one had a kite, he'd let it high up, and two loons crept through the lower hedge and stole a handful of the Dominie's tomatoes, and Peter took out his knife again, sharp, and waited for Jockie Elrick, they circled round each other, knives all ready, Peter said that Jockie Elrick was a Bulgar, and Jockie said that Peter was another, see, and then they both nodded "Wait till the morn" and separated, and you all held home, lasses trailing along in groups with their arms wound round one the other's shoulders, awful big, they petted you, you were over wearied to tell them you didn't like lasses, except maybe Rachel, she was fine.

She came down the Badymicks road behind you and Peter and Alick and you twice looked back, and saw her limp, and felt awful sorry, she looked dark herself in the fading light, would the folk in Africa that the lions ate be like her, would you say? And you looked back again and felt feared for her, and ran back to her side and took her hand, "I'll take care of you if the lions come." She said that was awful fine of you, but there weren't any in Scotland, she thought, you said "Maybe no, but this is the Howe" and held her hand down to Badymicks, she put her arms round you and kissed you then, liked it, but Peter and Alick had stopped and looked back and started mocking you. "Och, look at the lassies slobbering and kissing," and the Bulgars tormented you all the way home.

Mother asked how you'd gotten on, and you said "Och, fine" though you were so wearied, you fell asleep at the supper table and dreamt you were chasing Miss Clouston up the Howe with a gully knife in your hand, only it wasn't Miss Clouston but a great big beast, a lion from Africa, and it in its turn was chasing Rachel Camlin, pant and pant, you heard its great slobber, but you were gaining, gaining on it quick.

And then you woke up in the kitchen bed, dark in the early gliff of Spring morning, beside you Peter and Alick asleep, and far underfoot with shoggling surge the tide in the darkness taking its turn.

And still the rains of that Spring came down, at School every morning the bairns of the Howe sat and steamed like ill plates of porridge, and far and near through the tumbling runnels the water poured from the drooked lands to leave room for a fresh pelt coming at noon, piles of water tumbling and falling with a wheeling of rainbows and a cawing of gulls. To plough was to wade in mud to the knees, Arch Camlin digging up a bit of his moor fell into a bog and was nearly laired, he'd have died there but that Rachel was here, a Saturday, and ran for help to the figure of Dalsack across in his fields, ploughing and steaming with a blowing pair. Dalsack cried "What? Well, well, thet's gey coarse" and came stepping canny across the fields and looked down at Arch Camlin pinned in the hole under a weight of lever and broom. "Fegs, man, we'll need to howk you up out of that." Arch Camlin said he was awful kind, but wouldn't he first like a draw at his pipe? So Dalsack was a wee bit nipper then, and howked out Arch, clorted up and down from head to feet and over his head, shivering with cold.

Dalsack would have let him stagger off home, but Edith had seen the whole play from the kitchen and came running out and invited him in, "Dalsack, you old Bulgar, help the man to tirr." And she ran and made him a hot berry drink while Arch stripped off every clout he wore and got into a baggy old suit of Dalsack's, Rachel sitting by with her staring eyes, Edith big and bonny bustling around, caring nothing for naked men, seeing that Dalsack gave all his help. And Arch Camlin, coming away a bit later, thought back on the way that Edith behaved, 'od, yon was a funny-like way for a housekeeper to act with her lawful master, now.

He met in with Cruickshank from Moss Bank up the road and stopped to pass the news of the day, and said what he'd thought about Edith and Dalsack. Jim Cruickshank said "Damn't, and what's funny? She's a fine lass, Edith, but a whore for all. I'se warrant she warms the old sinner's bed."

Arch wouldn't have that, No, no, a fine lass, and Cruickshank said she was fine enough, but a whore by nature, she'd burn yet. So he drove off and Arch Camlin went home, Fannie trailing about like a wee dish cloth. He told her the tale of his time in the moor and all she said was "Faith, did you then? Eh me, and now I'll have to wash up your breeks and sark," b'god that was all that worried her.

So Arch took a bit of a stroll out that evening, walking canty along the dripping paths, and came to the high still ridge in the dripping silence of the cease of the rain, below the lights of Maiden were twinkling, he'd take a bit taik in about there, he thought. In the yard Geo Allison was watering the horses, the poor brutes skirted up over their dowps, and they stood and had a bit news a while till Maiden himself came out of the byre and cried "That you, Arch? Come away in." And into the kitchen Arch Camlin stepped, and who should be there, either nook of the fire than that Edith of Bogmuck and the soldier-childe, William, the ill-doing soldier-son of Moss Bank, looking chief as a cock and hen at each other, Mrs Stratoun tearing around at her work, the lads all snuggled in their beds already. Faith, it seemed the young Cruickshank hadn't the objections to Edith that his ill-tuned father had.

But Arch thought that little business of his and started with Maiden to take through hand the threshing mill that was coming to the village in a week or so, to Badymicks first, Bogmuck, and syne Maiden, then across the moor to Balhaggarty, from there along to Lamahip, Moss Bank said he would thresh his own. Edith and young Cruickshank sat and listened, young Cruickshank ignorant about things like this, he asked if they'd ever thought a time would come when a place like Maiden could drive its own thresher with electricity up from the sea? John Stratoun said "'Od, maybe we will, but we'll leave that over a year or two yet," giving his beard a bit of a stroke, ay, a dry soul, Maiden, Arch Camlin thought.

So out at last he went taiking home, and young Cruickshank and Edith rose to go with him, outside the rain had passed, stiffly blustering a great wind was darting up the Howe, they'd to bend their heads to the tingle and blow and fight their way to the long hedge-dripping track. At the break of the roads that led east and south, Arch Camlin cried out he'd take Edith home, but young Cruickshank said "Ho no, I'll come with you. Fine evening for a bit of a stroll, you know."

Faith, if that was the thing that he wanted he ended up with a sappier touch, looking back when he parted with them outside Bogmuck Arch Camlin saw him with Edith close up, tight in his arms as though he would mince her and kissing her lips in a fashion not decent, was that the way to behave to a lass that was good enough, but just a plain whore?

POSTSCRIPT

The novel, as the typescript was left, finishes at this enigmatic point. Already there are signs of haste in the typescript, signs like inconsistency of spelling and changes of mind, and near the end of the finished product, some signs of illness or inattention, words quite wrongly typed and not corrected. Pen corrections of the first-draft typescript are frequent in the early pages, then tail off completely towards the end.

What is interesting is not just the incomplete state of typescript, but the appendices which follow. If Gibbon had been composing at speed he could reasonably have been expected to go ahead full steam with his inspiration. Yet he finished the novel off neatly at the end of a sentence, and an episode, indeed those who write in this way will recognise the device of finishing at a point of interest where it will be relatively easy to bring the plot to life again after an interval.

There *are* signs that Gibbon meant the novel to be laid aside. The lack of corrections of the latter parts (work to be postponed till later), the frequent mistakes in typing not even back-spaced for obvious correction indicate haste and possibly poor health. But most significantly, the plot outlines which follow are all produced on the same typewriter, and cover incidents all completely outside the finished portion. These appendices were composed, we deduce, after the typescript was laid aside, as an indication of how work-in-progress was to be completed. They are not working documents, already partly incorporated in the plot, but all look to the future.

Two reasons suggest themselves. One, simply, is that Gibbon knew he had to put the novel in cold-storage (for reasons either of health or more pressing deadlines on other projects) and so jotted down in legible form some outlines of his original intentions, as a guide when he came back to this typescript. It would be a wholly natural thing to do.

Another, less obvious, reason is suggested by the fact that all the incidents relate to as-yet-unwritten parts of the plot. We know publishers were pushing Gibbon hard, and it is possible that in putting this project aside, he was typing up a fair-copy list of this kind to show to a publisher as a token of good intentions, and proof that he had run out not of inspiration, but of time. This is pure supposition, but the fair-copy nature of these postscripts does suggest that they were meant to be taken along with the completed portion to indicate a novel which could easily be brought to a publishable state, given a little more time. It would be a practical thing for a hard-pressed author in poor health to do, to buy a little relaxation of deadlines.

The reader who has followed the typescript through the finished and partly-corrected version will be struck with familiarity between *The Speak of the Mearns* and other Gibbon productions, obviously *Sunset Song*, less obviously the short story "Clay" and the incident of breaking in the field (and finding the buried prehistoric remains), the story "Smeddum" and the masterful farmer's wife. "The Land", the eloquent essay from *Scottish Scene*, finds much that is attractive about Scotland that tallies exactly with Keith's exact observations of the land, the birds, the seasons in Kinneff; Malcom Maudslay remembers experiences very like Keith's at the school he suffered in *The Thirteenth Disciple*. Yet the real similarities are to Blawearie and Kinraddie in *Sunset Song*, the obsessive gossip and interest in sexual peccadillo, the family of brothers with a quiet father and red-haired, hyperactive mother, the quiet book-ish observer beside the more active brothers — whether as Chris in *Sunset Song*, or Keith here, the author is drawing on autobiographical experience, his own experience in a crofting kitchen set aside from the farming interests of brothers and family, aiming for the school and the world outside, furthered by the energy of his mother, and almost

106

despite the opposition or the inertia of the rest of the rest of the community, always excepting the teachers and the school friends drawn very much from Gibbon's own childhood memory. Memorable, too, is the *Sunset Song* style with its careful mixture of Scots forms and English narrative base (defined by Gibbon in his "Literary Lights" essay in *Scottish Scene*), and its unique drift from autobiographical *parole intérieure* to the mind of the person hearing what is being said, to the overall consciousness of the community. The same multiple viewpoints which give the reader such delicate apprehension of the mind of Kinraddie give the reader of these pages something of Keith's infant apprehension of his community, and at the same time an adult's apprehension of a community far beyond the understanding of young Keith, with his inexperience of the world and of the female sex.

The shape of the finished novel, obviously, would have expanded Keith's observations from the intimacies of farm and father, family and friends to the world of books and experience, archaeology and travel, the towns and cities, and the world beyond; like James Leslie Mitchell coming from the farms and village school of Arbuthnott to national fame as Lewis Grassic Gibbon, so the central intelligence of *The Speak of the Mearns* would have expanded as incident succeeded incident, and in this controlled way would have grown to match the community voice of experience, then to pass it as Keith moved beyond the limitations of Maiden Castle and its village. That expansion had just begun with his emancipation from home to school; the further development must be the reader's responsibility, guided by the scanty notes Gibbon left.

The Speak of the Mearns would not have made Gibbon much more popular in his native countryside than did *Sunset Song*. Scandalous incident can at least be suggested to be tied to gossip and real-life incident, but as in the earlier work the close-knit community of obsessive interest gives marvellous cohesion to the work. The reader never pauses to think that Keith's world could never encompass this richness; rather the reader learns to move effortlessly in and out of Keith's world, till Keith himself comes of age. The technique here is obviously that of a man with a proven success in *Sunset Song*, deploying the same methods towards a fresh success in this sequel. The text is imperfect (though it has been lightly edited to remove obvious blemishes) but it suggests the secure ability to recall and to adapt, to marshall and control the speed of development which would very probably have made *The Speak of the Mearns* a success very much like *Sunset Song* — fascinating to those involved in Scottish rural life but not offended by local incident and allusion, infuriating to friends and family, and curiously, compulsively readable to those non-Scots who tried through Gibbon's technique to gain some insight into a vanishing world of Scottish rural activity. The novel's unfinished state is a real loss to the history of popular twentieth-century fiction in Scotland.

I.C.

APPENDIX

Lewis Grassic Gibbon's notes left at the end of the novel

1.   On the back of an envelope, Gibbon had scribbled:

Balhaggarty — Sam Paton & wife (Strachan) — two young sons, William & Peter
Moss Bank— Jim Cruickshank & huge wife. Two sons: Sandy the daftie & Joe the soldier
Auld Kirk — Rev James Dallas. Young, pretty wife
Free Kirk — Rev. Adam Smith. Housekeeper
Lamahip — Gunn; Bright wife; daughters Jean (religious) & Queen (mysterious)
Badymicks — Arch Camlin, his wife, & daughter Rachel.
Bogmuck — Dalsack & Edith
Howl [a name he sometimes applied in the draft to the village near Maiden Castle] — Munros, The Postmaster & son.

2.   *Development of Story:*

Sam Paton and his wife of BALHAGGARTY: Paton develops cancer. He was always full of wind and water. Mrs Paton sees more and more ghosts.

Jim Cruickshank and his wife of Moss Bank: They are drawn into the drama of Joseph's love of Edith, and finally flee the district. Towards the end, Cruickshank is out with a gun to kill Dalsack of Badymicks.

Reverend James Dallas of the Auld Kirk and his wife: The Rev grows more bitter and narrow, a sadist who ill-treats his wife and refuses her sexual intercourse. An afflicted imagination with the horrors of the Old Testament. Mrs Dallas ultimately consoles herself with young Munro of the Howe and his tormented sneers change to love.

Reverend Adam Smith of the Free Kirk summoned to console the mystic Queenie Gunn is confirmed in his dislike of all hatred not thoroughly dead. He goes digging in Stane Park and uncovers an ancient grave: the man done in with a blow at the back of the skull.

Stephen Gunn of Lamahip continues his lies. But in the end the old liar proves to have told the truth — some laird woman remembers him. At the Big House. Religious Jean with a baby. Queen goes to London and becomes a preacher.

Arch Camlin of Badymicks continues whistling and working. His complaining wife has another baby at which Mrs Stratoun attends.

111

Dalsack of Bogmuck and his housekeeper. Edith and Joe continue their flirtation. Edith reveals the father of her child as Dalsack. Marriage with Joe.

The Paralysed Pinto of Adam's Castle: His forester, Johnson, his keeper, McGrath. Hatred between the Stratouns and Pintos.

3. *Incidents:*

(1) Steam-mill. All the people of the Howe there. Water carrying. Chaff. Hum of the engine. Sights out beyond.
(2) Wedding of Joe and Edith.
(3) The horse that tumbled over the cliff: Geo Allison and Bess.
(4) Annual Games and Dance.
(5) Sunday School Picnic.
(6) Prize-giving.
(7) Tree-sawing in the woods — steading trees.
(8) James Dallas's discovery of his wife in Munro's arms.
(9) The hanging of Stephen Gunn.
(10) Burns' Nicht supper.

New Characters.
The Laird
Forester Johnson
Keeper McGrath
Gunn of Lamahip as old Scorgie plus old Hodge.